Harlequin
Presents..

ANNE HAMPSON

wings of night

HARLEQUIN BOOKS
toronto-winnipeg

© Anne Hampson 1971

Original hard cover edition published in 1971
by Mills & Boon Limited

SBN 373-70516-6
Harlequin Presents edition published August 1973

Printed in Canada.

CHAPTER ONE

IF ever he should have the opportunity of revenge, Lean had said, he would not hesitate to seize it.

His warning came to Melanie as she sat with her mother, having a cup of tea while awaiting the arrival of the taxi that would take her on the first stage of her journey to the Aegean island of Crete.

Melanie was seventeen when the handsome Leandros Angeli entered her life, seventeen and no different from the frivolous and pleasure-seeking crowd with which she mixed. Lean was twenty-four and as serious as Melanie was gay. Holidaying in England, he had fallen in love with Melanie on sight and within a fortnight they were engaged. As Melanie's parents and younger brother were also on holiday they did not meet Lean, for he had to return to Crete where he owned several hotels inherited from his father. But he promised to be back in a month's time, when he would meet her parents and arrangements would be made for the wedding. Melanie by this time was fully occupied with someone else and with the heartlessness of youth she gave Lean back his ring.

It was then that she met a totally different man, discovering to her cost the savagery and sense of possession so characteristic of the average Greek male. He had left her trembling, nursing her bruises and squirming under his bitter invective. Towering above her, his eyes black pools of hate, he had finally uttered the warning that now hung so heavily upon her.

What tricks fate did play! For her brother had recently robbed Lean's sister of a thousand pounds, and because of this Melanie found herself completely in the

5

power of the man who, seven years previously, had sworn dark vengeance upon her.

'I'm so dreadfully worried about you.' Her mother's distressed voice broke into Melanie's thoughts and she glanced up. 'You're literally selling yourself into slavery. How is this man going to treat you?'

Melanie considered that, and her face lost a little more of its colour.

'In the way he firmly believes I deserve to be treated,' she replied quietly at length. 'I'm not expecting any quarter from Lean Angeli.'

'He's hateful – presenting you with an ultimatum like this! He knows it's your brother's crime!'

Melanie hesitated. As she had never mentioned her brief engagement, her mother could not know that Gerard's debt was a welcome tool providing Lean with the means of revenge. And so to her his terms must appear exceedingly harsh.

'I had some of the money,' Melanie reminded her. 'In Lean's opinion that makes me equally blameworthy.' She brought into focus the formidable features of Lean as she had seen him last week. Had Gerard met the brother first he would undoubtedly have had second thoughts about duping the sweet and trusting little Eleni.

'You didn't know how Gerard came by the money, though. He should have made allowances for that.'

Gerard had won two hundred pounds on the football pools, he had lied, suggesting that he and Melanie buy a second-hand car between them. She had eagerly agreed, unaware of his treachery, or that the two hundred pounds was what remained after the clearing of his gambling debts.

'I don't believe the fact registered,' Melanie said, recalling how Lean had promptly silenced her every attempt at speech. 'And it wouldn't have influenced

6

him if it had.'

'He's inhuman, demanding payment in this way. It's going to take years!'

About two years, Melanie reckoned, appalled at the prospect. Until the money was repaid she must work in one of Lean's hotels, the whole of her salary each month being set against the debt.

'Better this way than prosecution,' she returned flatly.

'You really believe he'd have carried out his threat?'

'I'm sure of it. He'd have prosecuted Gerard, and I'd have been involved too, having received some of the money. It would have killed Father.'

Her mother found a handkerchief and rubbed her eyes.

'That my son could have brought such disgrace upon us!' She looked at Melanie, pain in her glance. 'Where have we slipped up – your father and I?'

'You're not to blame; it was the company he kept.' An involuntary shudder passed through Melanie's slender body at the memory of the shocks she and her parents had received. She felt the two events which would remain with her for the rest of her life were the confession of her brother and the visit from Lean last week.

Gerard had come in looking white and ill. Full of concern, Mrs. Rawson had asked him what was wrong. He was in dreadful trouble, Gerard had said, and they had all listened while he told them of the gambling debts, of the girl to whom he had become engaged solely to get his hands on her money – and whom he had since jilted – and the brother who was even now on his way to England intent on restitution.

'You've been gambling?' faltered Melanie, while her mother just looked on in rather frightened disbelief.

Her father, she noticed with a frown, had sunk into the chair, the blue tinge on his lips providing evidence that his heart was giving him trouble.

Gerard nodded sullenly.

'I owed eight hundred and was desperate. This girl – she's Greek – had fallen for me; I knew she had money, so I got engaged. Then I asked her for a thousand—'

'A thousand!' his mother cried, beginning to tremble from head to foot. 'A thousand pounds?'

He shrugged and told her sulkily that the girl could well afford it.

'Gerard,' put in Melanie, unable to take in this change in her brother, 'do you know what you're saying?'

'All right, I shouldn't have taken her money – and believe me, I wish I hadn't, for this brother of hers is coming to see me.'

His father asked quietly,

'What tale did you tell this girl in order to get the money from her?'

'I said it was her share of the down payment on a house – I'd already shown her a house and she liked it. I was to pay a thousand as well, I told her.'

'You lied like that to a girl who loved you?' Mrs. Rawson seemed on the verge of collapse. 'You duped her, robbed her of all that money?'

'What else could I do? But she never even mentioned a brother – and now he's coming— What am I to do! Eleni says he'll kill me!'

'Eleni!' Lean had had a young sister called Eleni. His mother, an educated and enlightened woman, had insisted on an education for her daughter comparable to that of her son, and so, Lean had said, Eleni would eventually come to a university in England. Aware of her parents' curiosity, Melanie became guarded. 'That's a fairly common name in Greece. Er – what's the brother's name?'

'Leandros.'

Leandros. . . . Melanie's pulse fluttered and her voice trembled slightly as she inquired about the surname. But somehow she did not need to be told it was Angeli. She was as white as Gerard as she said,

'When are you expecting the brother?'

'Eleni says he'll be here tomorrow.'

'You're still seeing this girl, then?' his father put in, his lined face pale and drawn.

'She came into the office, and fairly shouted at me, so everyone could hear—' he broke off, mopping his brow. 'She's always been so timid and meek – the way you expect all Greek girls to be – and I thought I'd have no trouble – but to go and cable her brother! I couldn't believe it!'

His father's expression changed to one of contempt.

'You expected to rob this girl of a thousand pounds and have no trouble? My son, you've a lot to learn. Naturally she'd enlist the aid of her people. Well, what are your intentions?'

'I haven't a penny!' He looked at his sister almost accusingly. 'You had the last two hundred for the car.'

'I. . . .' Melanie felt quite sick. She had received stolen money . . . and to buy a car of all things. 'It must be sold,' she said emphatically. 'Also, this money must be available when Lean – wh-when this man arrives. We'll have to find the money somehow.' But she spoke wildly, and this was impressed upon her by her father saying quietly,

'Find a thousand pounds, Melanie? Where would we obtain a sum like that?' He glanced at her significantly and she bit her lip. He had been an invalid for five years, his heart complaint preventing him from taking

9

on even the lightest of work.

'We must get it,' she returned, desperately trying to quell the fear that was slowly spreading over her as she recalled that parting from Lean seven years ago. He had been so filled with black vindictiveness, and although her common sense told her he would not harbour it all this time, some other instinct convinced her that he would harbour it for ever.

Of course they could not find so large a sum, and Gerard, thoroughly scared of meeting the brother of the girl he had duped, made his escape by running off to stay with some friends in the north of Scotland, taking the car with him.

This cowardly action, coming immediately upon his confession, brought on one of Mr. Rawson's heart attacks, and as it was rather more severe than normal Melanie rang the doctor and within half an hour of his arrival Mr. Rawson was in the ambulance and on his way to hospital, accompanied by his wife.

'How can I leave you to face that man alone?' she had cried while waiting for the ambulance. 'And yet I must go with your father.'

'Certainly you must.' Despite her trepidation Melanie forced a smile. 'I'll be quite all right; he can't eat me.'

Lean arrived an hour later, and with throbbing pulse and legs that almost refused to function she managed to reach the door and open it. The change in him struck her forcibly, making her forget for a few seconds the reason for his visit. Those seven years had matured him, brought to his features character lines that gave them an added quality of arrogance and superiority. He had about him a remoteness and inaccessibility that seemed in themselves to answer her silent question, 'Is he married?' She knew instinctively that he had no wife, sensed that here was a man so aloof and unbending that the casual affair, conducted with indifference and a total lack of affection, was all in which he would ever indulge. For this was not the Lean she had known, the boy who had laughed with her, who had lavished on her adoring glances and tender kisses, giving her a wealth of love until that terrifying demonstration on the day she returned his ring. Melanie had never been quite the same since then. The encounter had chastened her, brought home to her the futility of the life she led – the gay round and empty pleasures, the lack of fulfilment. With a new determination she had resolved to take life seriously; she had studied for a career and had achieved what had hitherto been a half-hearted ambition, that of working for one of London's top dress designers.

'The taxi's here. Darling, are you really going?' Jerked back to the present by her mother's anxious voice, Melanie breathed a sigh of relief. For she had no desire to live again in thought that half hour she had spent with Lean, to suffer the lash of his tongue or shiver under the icy condemnation of his gaze. He allowed her speech only to answer his questions. On his inquiring if it were true that she had used some of the money to buy a car she had been forced to say yes; on his demand for the immediate return of the money she had been forced to own that this was not possible.

And then had come the most odd expression to Lean's face, followed by the threat of prosecution . . . and finally, the ultimatum.

'Certainly I'm going, Mother.' She stood up, pale but resolute. 'There's no other way.' She forced a smile as she added, 'I imagine it will be two years at most, and that isn't a lifetime.'

'I hope it is only two years – but you said he wouldn't commit himself as to your salary.'

Yes, that had certainly troubled Melanie at the time,

and it still did trouble her, for she was completely at his mercy.

'I should imagine he'll give me a fair deal, paying me what I'm worth.'

'But you don't even know what sort of a job you're being given.'

'Something like a receptionist, I should think. And although wages are low in Greece he surely won't offer me less than five hundred a year. I'll have my food and board, so I should be able to save practically all of it.'

'Five hundred a year – and what you've given up!'

Melanie's face clouded as she thought of her job – and her boss, the handsome young dress designer from whom she would soon have received a proposal of marriage. Richard Melton's initial interest had been purely mercenary, for Melanie was almost as clever as he and often Richard would bask in the glory that should have been hers. Melanie harboured no resentment over this, because not only had he hinted at a partnership, but recently he had begun taking her about and it was clear he was becoming personally involved. There were times when to be his wife was all that Melanie desired – but on other occasions she would have the most disturbing doubts. Richard's angry amazement on learning she was to leave him was something else on which Melanie had no wish to dwell. On her absolute refusal to explain he had emphatically declared he would visit her in Crete during the summer and discover for himself what this was all about.

'I'll find another post just as good when I return,' she said, with more optimism than she felt. 'Don't look so worried, pet. I'm not a baby; I can take care of myself.'

'I wish I'd been here to see this man. You haven't said much about him at all.' The wide brown eyes, so like her daughter's, held an expression that actually brought a laugh to Melanie's lips.

'He has no dark and sinister intentions, if that's what you're fearing. Lean Angeli wouldn't ever be interested in me in that sort of way.'

'No ... I suppose you're right, but do take care, darling.' Resignedly she followed Melanie to the door. 'We've discussed it so much that there's nothing more to be said.'

'And no time, even if there were.' Melanie then spoke to the taxi driver, indicating the suitcases standing in the hall. They were deposited in the boot and seconds later Melanie was kissing her mother goodbye. A shaky little laugh was produced in an effort to keep back the tears. 'I feel rather like one of the Athenian maidens who had to be sacrificed to the savage monster, the Minotaur of Crete—'

'Melanie, don't joke about it!'

'I'm sorry.' Genuine distress entered Melanie's eyes as she looked into her mother's face. 'You mustn't worry about me; I shall be quite safe.'

'Write soon,' Mrs. Rawson begged, ignoring Melanie's remarks. 'Immediately you arrive there – and tell me all that's happening.'

After promising to do that Melanie kissed her mother again and went down the steps to the waiting taxi.

With the Gulf of Athens left behind there was little to be seen, although Melanie caught a glimpse of Milos, the island on which the famous Venus de Milo was found. From this height it appeared treeless, and its landscape dull and uninteresting. Crete was very different, with its mountains shining like burnished bronze as the sun blazed down from a sky of vivid blue. The cubic houses, so typical of the East, looked like

13

rows of white boxes, with occasionally one having fallen out of line to perch itself in isolation on the mountainside. Melanie looked down with interest, eager to forget for a while the real reason for her being here. Somewhere among those mountains was the high peak of Mount Ida, birthplace of the mighty Zeus, supreme ruler of all the pagan gods of Greece. And somewhere was the immense Palace of Minos, the Labyrinth in which had dwelt the monster, half bull, half man, to whom had been sent as tribute every ninth year seven of the fairest maids of Athens, and seven of its noblest youths.

Perhaps, thought Melanie as the plane circled over the outskirts of Heraklion, there would be compensations. She could explore, putting to careful use her small savings, all of which she had brought with her in the form of traveller's cheques. With this idea came the question as to how much time off she would be allowed. Melanie had a shrewd suspicion that Lean would drive her hard, but at least she must have two days a week for herself, she reasonably concluded.

Lean was waiting at the airport and they made a silent journey in his car to the Hotel Avra at Heraklion. The sun was dropping and in its slanting rays the mountains were being turned from bronze to rust interspersed with greys and browns as the naked crags threw shadows into the valleys down below.

The Avra was the largest and most luxurious hotel in Crete, with every apartment having its own bathroom and balcony. There was air-conditioning and central heating, a luxurious restaurant and bar and a swimming pool illuminated from below.

Lean himself took Melanie to her room. It was in the roof, and contained a single iron bedstead with a dull grey cover, a marble-topped washing stand with drawers and a wardrobe that appeared to have been constructed out of odd scraps of wood. The floor was of bare stone and there was not even a small rug by the bed. The window, set higher than Melanie's head, was a mere slit in the wall through which it grudgingly allowed a ray of light to pass.

Melanie stood on the threshold, holding both her suitcases, and gasping inwardly as the intentions of this man impressed themselves upon her. This was no more than a prison cell!

She turned; Lean was close behind, and as she looked up at him, noting the mingling of cruelty and triumph in his eyes, she thought for a moment of his ancestors, those pagans who had lived for battle and the glorious death. And, later, the Cretans had continued their merciless slaughter – living as they did in constant revolt against the Saracens, the Venetians and the Turks. Right down through their history there had been someone to hate ... but today there was no one, and so perhaps there existed a vacuum in the life of the average Cretan ... perhaps he preferred to have an enemy at hand, a victim to torture and subdue.

Walking slowly into the centre of the room, Melanie stopped, taking in the drab ceiling and stone-coloured walls before saying, her low sweet voice edged with disbelief,

'This is to be my room – for two years?'

'Two years? What makes you think the debt will be cleared in two years?'

Putting down the suitcases, one on either side of her, Melanie turned, a fluttering sensation in the pit of her stomach.

'I estimated it would take two years,' she faltered, and Lean's brows rose a fraction.

'Then I'm afraid your estimate was well out. My estimate is that it will take at least twice that long.'

'Four years!' she gasped, spreading her hands in a

gesture of disgust. 'I'm not staying in this place for four years!'

His dark brows rose a little higher.

'I'm afraid you'll have to, for it's all you're going to get.' He moved further into the room. 'I shouldn't let it trouble you overmuch; you'll merely be sleeping here.'

The inference took the colour from her cheeks.

'If you'll tell me my hours, and my salary, then I shall know where I stand.'

For a moment he returned no answer, but stood looking at her, examining every feature, every line and curve.

'Your hours,' he informed her at length, 'will be from six in the morning till eight at night, with Sunday off. Your wage will be in accordance with the rate for a bedroom maid—'

'A *what*!'

'I believe you heard me.' Lean stifled a yawn. 'You appear to have had some other post in mind?'

Melanie swallowed hard.

'I expected a better post, certainly.'

'Such as?'

'Well ... I did think of a receptionist, or something.'

'You *were* aiming high.' The sneer in his voice was almost imperceptible; the amusement in his glance was much more apparent. 'I put my staff into work which I consider suitable to their particular level, and it was my original intention to put you in the kitchen, where you would be engaged in work like washing up and cleaning floors. However, I've spared you that supreme humiliation and – upgraded you, as it were.' He paused to watch with satisfaction the colour mounting her cheeks. 'Incidentally, the receptionist here is English. Being next in command to me, she is naturally your superior. You'll take all your orders from her.'

A great sigh left Melanie's lips. She reflected on their brief courtship, and wondered how she would have fared had she married this man. *This* man? No, he was no longer the man who had fallen so madly in love with her.

'You've changed, Lean – how you've changed!' She spoke her thoughts aloud, and guessed by his altered expression that the words had revived a memory.

'So have you, Melanie.' His eyes once more examined her face. 'You're older – but just as beautiful, I'll grant you that. The same hair of burnished gold, the same sweeping lashes—' Before she could grasp his intention he had flicked a careless finger across one blushing cheek. 'The same delicate features so charmingly fashioned, the same captivating lips and peach-tinted skin—' He broke off and a harsh laugh echoed through the sparsely furnished room. 'An entrancing veneer, Melanie, to hide the ugliness beneath.' His dark eyes flickered over her before coming to rest insultingly on the tender curves of her breast. 'The same perfectly proportioned figure, but rather more – er – rounded.'

'Lean,' said Melanie quietly after a small hesitation, 'I have of necessity to work for you, but there was nothing in our agreement about your having the right to insult me. I believe I'm entitled to some small respect from you.'

At that his eyes kindled dangerously.

'Speaking of respect,' he countered in a soft and warning tone, 'you'll address me by my surname. I of course shall call you by your first name, as I do with the other menials in my employ.'

Melanie's blood boiled. She could never tolerate this man for four years – four years! She shook her head, realized Lean had noticed the movement and informed him that her brother would have to contribute, in which case the debt would most probably be paid off within the two years she had at first mentioned.

'His studies were finished only six months ago,' she went on in a low and faintly husky tone, 'so at present he isn't earning much. But immediately he is I shall ask him to make monthly payments to you.' Lean was at the other side of the room, casually glancing through the slit from which came a feeble ray of the dying sun. Melanie watched him in profile, saw the hard inflexible line, like some silhouette of a statue carved in granite, and the shades of fear darkened her eyes even before he turned and spoke.

'I'm not willing to be paid in any other way than the one I stipulated. You made a bargain with me and you'll abide by it—'

'I didn't expect to be paid a pittance for my work!'

'I repeat,' he returned with maddening calm, 'you'll be paid the rate for the job.'

'You didn't tell me I was to be a – a bedroom maid. I never expected to be employed in a menial task like that!' Lean stared at her with acute disdain, but not a muscle moved on his cold and arrogant face.

'I remarked that I place my staff in the position suited to them. In my opinion you're fit only for the lowest work, so you had better not complain, otherwise I might change my mind and relegate you to the kitchen.'

She turned angrily – and knocked one of her suit-cases over. Lean looked at her rather in the way he might have looked at a worm.

'I hate you,' she breathed, clenching her fists. 'This diabolical method of revenge – only someone like you could devise it! It proves just how different your people are from mine!' She was actually hinting that she was glad she had not married him and to her satisfaction she at last succeeded in arousing in him some emotion, for the dark colour crept slowly under the deep mahogany of his skin. But to her surprise and disappointment his voice maintained its calm and even accents as he said,

'We differ from your people, I agree. We could never, for instance, think up such a dastardly method of robbing a young and trusting girl.' Contemptuously his eyes flickered over her face. 'You will take your meals in the kitchen,' he said, abruptly changing the subject. 'Tea will be ready in a few minutes. You'll report for duty at six in the morning, but you had better see Miss Newson this evening before she goes off duty. One of the kitchen staff will take you to her office.'

He closed the door quietly behind him and Melanie stood looking at it for a long while, her spirits sinking lower and lower with every moment that passed. She had said she expected no quarter – but she had expected justice. With another dismal examination of her surroundings, she switched on the light and began to unpack, putting her clothes away in the wardrobe and the drawers. A cell. . . . She had seen pictures of prison cells, and they were far more comfortable than this!

Four years! Did he think she would be so timid and docile as to slave for him for four years? Two years was the period to which she had resigned herself and two years it would be. Gerard would have to find some of the money, and Lean would have to accept it. He could scarcely prosecute if the money was there for him to take.

Her unpacking finished, Melanie picked up her towel and went in search of the bathroom. It was as drab and antiquated as her bedroom and a frown of perplexity settled on her brow. How came this part of the hotel to be so different from the luxury below? The window offering a little more scope than that in her room, she stood on the end of the bath and, opening the shutters, peered out to examine the exterior of the building. And then she understood. This had been a very old house and on to it had been added the main building of the hotel. The lower part of this building had been modernized, and Melanie was to discover that this top floor had until recently been used as a storage place for anything that didn't happen to be required downstairs.

After washing her face and brushing her hair, Melanie left the room. She was eyed with considerable curiosity when at last she managed to locate the kitchen. But not one of the women could speak a word of English. However, they eventually grasped what she wanted and one of them shyly led her out of the domestic quarters and along a carpeted corridor, stopping at a door near the end and indicating that this was Miss Newson's office.

Melanie knocked and entered. She had no idea what she expected, but she was certainly not prepared to see a girl as beautiful as Olga Newson. The girl had poise too, and there was a certain arrogance in the way her fair head was set on her tanned and shapely shoulders. She glanced up from some papers she was perusing, and her blue eyes swept over Melanie with a rather curious interest before she said in a low and drawling tone,

'You're Melanie, the new room maid. Mr. Angeli said you'd be in to see me.' She gave an indifferent nod indicating one of the chairs and added, 'You may sit down.'

Melanie's temper rose, but she sat down, opposite to Olga Newson, and thought of the respect that had been hers when she herself was second in command – to Richard Melton.

'Lean – Mr. Angeli said I had to give you your instructions,' Olga went on, idly fingering one of the papers on her desk. 'But as we have another English room maid here – Sandra Jenkins – I decided it would be simpler all round if I handed you over to her. I've already told her about you and you'll see her in the kitchen at six o'clock tomorrow morning. She'll show you what you must do.'

To Melanie it seemed the height of bad manners for Olga Newson not to take the trouble to introduce her to this Sandra and she said, rather stiffly,

'You won't be there in the morning?'

'At six o'clock!' Olga's glance swept haughtily over her. 'My dear girl, I'm not even awake at that time!'

Melanie stood up, quivering with rage.

'Is that all, Miss Newson?' she inquired, flashing the girl a glance as arrogant as her own. 'If so, I'll not take up any more of your time.'

Olga gasped unbelievingly as she came forward in her chair.

'Have you forgotten I'm your superior?' she asked softly.

'I could scarcely forget that, Miss Newson.'

The other girl's mouth compressed and she seemed lost for words. The timid Greek women, grateful to be working in the hotel, would in all probability grovel to this woman, thought Melanie, so this present experience would be quite new to her.

'I shall have to report this insolence to Mr. Angeli,' Olga snapped at length, and then she added in a warning tone, 'It wouldn't surprise me if he dismisses you from his service even before you've started work.'

'It wouldn't?' A smile of sardonic amusement

touched the corners of Melanie's mouth. 'It would certainly surprise me, Miss Newson,' she said, and without waiting to see what effect that had on the other girl she turned and left the room.

CHAPTER TWO

Kyrios the porter came to Melanie the following morning at ten o'clock.

'Mr. Leandros, he want to see you – in his office.'

'Thank you.' She finished making the bed, put a duster on the furniture and then went down to the ground floor, and to the room which Sandra had earlier informed her was Lean's office.

In answer to her knock she was invited to enter. Lean stood by the window; she saw him in profile and involuntarily caught her breath, for there was about him a supreme and noble quality that seemed to raise him far above any other man she had ever known. One hand was thrust into his pocket and he looked out on to the harbour, with its impressive Venetian castle and its tawny weathered bastions invading a sea of bright metallic blue.

'You wished to see me?' A hint of tartness in her voice, for he just kept her standing there, completely ignoring her.

Presently he turned, raked her with a lofty glance and then looked at the clock on the wall.

'I sent for you ten minutes ago,' he said in soft and measured tones. 'What kept you?'

Melanie bristled.

'I finished what I was doing.'

'Then in future – don't.' Moving into the centre of the room he stood with his hand resting on the back of the chair by his desk. 'When I send for you you'll obey the summons immediately.' An emphasis on the last four words brought out his accent. Slight, it was, and could have been attractive had his voice not been edged with this cold superiority. 'I'm informed that during your interview with Miss Newson last evening your manner was insolent, to say the least.'

Anger brought a sparkle to Melanie's eyes and two bright spots of colour to her cheeks.

'She wasn't particularly polite to me.' Melanie endeavoured to keep the fury out of her voice, but failed, and her employer's eyes narrowed dangerously.

'She was there to give you your orders, not indulge in friendly conversation. In future you'll refrain from answering her back. Is that clear?'

Melanie drew a deep breath and her eyes met his, militantly.

'I think, Mr. Angeli, that we should understand each other right at the beginning, in order to avoid the development of any deeper animosity than already exists between us—'

'You needn't trouble your head about that,' he softly interrupted. 'For my part, there could be no deterioration in my opinion of you. It's as low as it can be.' The quiet contempt went strangely deep as Melanie recalled the respect she had always been afforded at her work – the respect and admiration.

'Perhaps you'll come to the point and tell me why I'm here,' she requested curtly, determined to keep her temper. 'I'm sure neither of us has any desire to remain in one another's company longer than is necessary.'

Dark colour rising portrayed his anger; his voice when he spoke was like cold steel.

'I think you've forgotten why you're in Greece at all, so I'll refresh your memory. You and your brother plotted to rob my sister—'

'I must correct you there—'

Lean's hand left the chair and Melanie actually jumped as it came down flatly on the desk.

'Don't interrupt me when I'm speaking! It behoves

24

you to know your place here! As I said, you and your brother plotted to rob a young and trusting girl.' He stopped and his black eyes spared her none of the contempt he felt for her. 'It was your misfortune that that girl happened to be my sister. You're here to undergo a period of punishment, and to make retribution. It may interest you to know,' he added as an afterthought, 'that I've repaid my sister the money and you now owe it to me.'

The colour had left Melanie's face and the pallor added a sort of enchantment to the clear skin and contrasted rather flatteringly with the hazel-brown of her eyes. To think that she had once been engaged to this man, had thrilled to his kisses – yes, she recollected, his passionate, rather frightening lovemaking had excited her in a way she had never really forgotten. Other kisses she had received, but they had left her cold; even Richard had failed to awaken any response in her, and she supposed that was the reason for her doubts as to how she would respond to his proposal of marriage.

Melanie's thoughts were brought back to the present as her employer drew an impatient breath.

'You're really punishing me for – for that other.' The statement was forced from her and Lean's eyes glinted. Did he hate being reminded of the past? she wondered, only now fully appreciating the depth of the humiliation to which he had been subjected. To her, living on the surface, indulging in a gay and barren round of pleasure, the appearance of Lean on the scene had come as a diversion. Tall and handsome, with even then a masterful, commanding personality that thrilled even while it intimidated, he was different. He was from the mysterious East and all her girl friends wove a veil of romance around him and envied her. His swift proposal of marriage was flattering and had sent her soaring into the clouds. But to Melanie at that time there was nothing really solid in her affair with Lean and even though she received his ring the idea of marriage remained distant and unreal.

Greece, of which he spoke with pride and enthusiasm, was as vague as the idea of marriage, Melanie seeing Lean's country as a barbaric land of temples and gods where in the dim and distant past wild pagan rites had been conducted beneath the shadow of towering heights such as the massifs of Parnassus and Mount Helicon. A land where the mighty Zeus had commanded an island to appear out of the sea, to provide a birthplace for his son Apollo, or where from the rocks a spring could miraculously gush forth simply because Pegasus had struck the spot on landing from the skies. It was a land shrouded in mystery, as obscure as the vision of a future spent with this dark and passionate Greek, and Melanie did in fact experience a feeling of relief on deciding to return her fiancé's ring. She had given not a thought to his reaction, having no knowledge of the passions and emotions and depth of sensitivity of the Greeks. Similarly, she knew nothing of their inherent ruthlessness and inhumanity, or of the lengths to which they would go to avenge an insult or a slight.

But many times since she had grown older, adopting a more serious and realistic attitude towards life, Melanie had known the pangs of shame and contrition at the thoughtlessness of her behaviour. She would not treat an engagement so lightly now. And that was why she experienced such uncertainty whenever the idea of a proposal of marriage from Richard should cross her mind.

'I warned you,' admitted Lean, breaking into her thoughts, 'that if ever the opportunity of revenge should be presented to me, I should not hesitate to seize it. Yes, I am punishing you for that other crime; I consider you should be chastened, made to realize that an engagement is no transient interlude in a life reduced to boredom by its sheer lack of purpose.' The gravity of his words, coupled with his nobility of bearing, had the effect of instilling into her a feeling of inferiority and blame. He was so dignified and aloof, looking down at her from an incredible height. Who was it who said that a noble Cretan could possess an eye and an air that could make the most imperious Spanish grandee seem like an effeminate poseur?

'The – our engagement – you must have – have—' She hesitated, lowering her head. 'You must have got over it by now?'

He stiffened, but gave no sign that her words had affected him emotionally.

'I'm no longer eating my heart out,' he told her with a glance of cold derision. 'Not for a woman as completely unworthy as you. However,' he added in an explanatory tone, 'were you more closely acquainted with the character of my people you would not be surprised at my desire for revenge. We do not suffer insults lightly. I mean to punish you, and to prolong that punishment over as great a period as I can.'

Melanie's throat felt blocked and dry. How long must she remain in this man's power?

'That is something I want to speak to you about, Le— Mr. Angeli. I'm writing to my brother; he must contribute to the paying off of this debt. If he does produce some money you'll have to accept it.'

'You expect your brother to contribute?' His fine brows lifted sceptically. 'You're far too optimistic, I'm afraid.'

'I'll get the money somehow!' she flared, even while she was plunged into despair by his words. 'I don't care how I do it, but I'll find some way of supplementing my wages!' Without waiting for any other response to that Melanie almost ran from the room, little knowing that the time would come when she would bitterly regret having uttered those words.

Sandra was brushing the landing when Melanie returned to the first floor where her rooms were situated.

'Kyrios said the boss had sent for you?' Sandra stood embracing the brush handle as if she were holding it for support, and looked inquiringly at Melanie.

'It was nothing important.' Melanie would have passed on, but Sandra spoke again.

'What do you think of him? Cold as an image . . . but what a stunner!' A rather soulful expression replaced the twinkle in her eyes and Melanie had to smile. To her surprise Sandra had turned out to be quite well educated – and unusual. At the age of twenty-one she had already worked her way through Europe; it was her intention to see the world before settling down, she had told Melanie, adding that she was staying in Crete only long enough to earn the money for a trip to Egypt where she hoped to renew the acquaintance with an Arab she had met when in Rome.

'Fell for him right away – whoosh!' she confessed, but with a laugh. 'Perhaps I'll feel quite differently when I see him again—' She broke off, shrugging. 'What does it matter? He'll come in useful in showing me around.' She had gone on to say she was exploring the island at the same time as saving for the trip, and Melanie had wondered just how much exploring one could do with only one day a week off, part of which must of necessity be taken up with such chores as cleaning out one's room and washing and ironing one's clothes. But Melanie did not go into this, for Sandra was telling her her duties, explaining that the day began with the cleaning of the rooms downstairs, the brushing of verandahs and the setting out of deck chairs both on these verandahs and in the gardens.

'Yes . . . a real stunner,' Sandra repeated dreamily as she began brushing the landing again. 'I wonder what's between him and his beautiful secretary, or whatever she is. Can't stand her – far too supercilious and full of her own importance; suits him, though, for he can make you feel like a worm if the fit takes him.'

'You think . . . there's something between them?'

Sandra cast her a sly glance from under her lashes.

'You bet your life there is!' She laughed in a rather condescending, yet good-humoured way. 'It's easy to see you haven't much knowledge of the Greeks. Women are as necessary to them as food!'

Melanie flushed, but managed to say,

'They'll marry eventually, you think?'

Sandra pursed her lips and considered this.

'Could do, I suppose, but Greeks don't usually marry their pillow friends. They're merely diversions *until* marriage. You see,' she went on to explain, 'Greek girls are pure – have to be, or they'd never get husbands – so the men naturally have affairs with women who are not particularly concerned about marriage. With our boss it might be different because Olga's English and for that reason he might be regarding her in an altogether different light from that in which he would regard one of his own women.'

'How old do you think she is?' Melanie frowned as she asked the question. Why should she be interested in Olga's age?

'Twenty-eight or nine–'

'What are you two girls supposed to be doing?' The imperious voice of Olga Newson cut Sandra short and she once again returned to her task of brushing the landing. 'You're not paid to stand here gossiping all day! Melanie, where are you supposed to be?'

For a moment temper choked the words in Melanie's throat, and even when she did speak her voice trembled with fury.

'In the bedroom.'

'What number?'

'Fourteen.'

'You've done the others?'

'Some of the people have not yet gone out.'

'You've done this one?' Sandra was standing by the door of room eight and Melanie nodded stiffly. 'Then I'll take a look at it.'

'Bitch!' Sandra hissed between her teeth. 'She'll find some dust, I'm warning you. Or else you'll not have polished the bath taps to her liking.'

'Melanie, come here!'

'Told you!' Sandra grinned, but made a gesture with her thumb. 'Better go, and make it snappy. She's in one of her foul moods by the sound of things.'

'Is something wrong?' Melanie stood by the door, pale but dignified, her words and manner bringing an arrogant and warning light to Olga Newson's eyes. She left unsaid any complaint for the moment as she came forward and stood very close to Melanie.

'I don't like your attitude, miss,' she snapped. 'Mr. Angeli has informed you of my position here?'

Ignoring that, Melanie asked again if there were anything wrong.

'If so,' she added quietly, 'kindly tell me what it is and I'll proceed to put it right.'

'You—' Olga's lips compressed and her face went red. 'I'll speak to Mr. Angeli again about you! I'm not tolerating your insolence; I'll have you sacked!' She swung round and waved her arm in an all-embracing gesture. 'This room's a positive disgrace. Get it cleaned – at once!'

'She seems to have it in for you,' observed Sandra a

few days later when they were having their lunch in the corner of the garden which Lean had fenced off and reserved for the use of his staff.

'We didn't make a very amicable start,' admitted Melanie. 'She rubbed me up the wrong way and I retaliated.'

A curious glance from Sandra before she said,

'You answered her back?'

'Certainly.'

Reaching for a sandwich, Sandra began nibbling it, although her eyes were fixed on Melanie with an odd expression in their depths.

'No one answers Olga Newson back without suffering for it. She must have reported you to the boss.'

'She did – and said I'd probably be dismissed even before I started.'

'And you weren't . . .' Sandra nibbled thoughtfully, her blue eyes still fixed on Melanie's face. 'That room you're in,' she began tentatively. 'I can't make out why you're up there, cut off from everyone, in such an uncomfortable apartment.' Not a question, and Melanie picked up her coffee and took a drink, her attention apparently on the café on the other side of the road. The sight was now familiar – sprawling men on the verge of sleep; finger-beads clicking, hookah pipes, minute cups of coffee and trik-trak. . . . Such was the life of the average Greek male.

'I expect there was no other room to give me,' submitted Melanie at length, and a little twist of Sandra's head denoted her surprise.

'There's the room along from me, you know of it. It's lovely, with a much better view than mine. And it's for the staff; an English girl had it, but she was on the move like me and left for the Holy Land just after I came. It's been vacant ever since.' A pause, but as

Melanie's attention returned to the café opposite
Sandra went on, 'I haven't asked you any questions
because I knew you'd resent it, but it doesn't say I'm
not curious.' Melanie offered no enlightenment and
Sandra ventured, eyeing her with an odd expression,
'What's the mystery?'

'Mystery?' In only five days a friendship had sprung
up between the two girls, and Melanie had begun to
wonder just how long it would be before she was faced
with the choice of answering Sandra's questions or
risking a coolness entering into their relationship. For
whereas Sandra had unfolded to Melanie practically
the whole of her life's history, Melanie had preserved
an attitude of reticence about her home and her past
and the reason for her being here. Inevitably questions
must come, but even though Melanie expected them
she remained undecided as to her answers. 'I
don't know what you mean?'

Sandra shrugged, but not with resignation, for she
said, in her usual good-humoured tones,

'I'm going to ask you a question, Melanie, and if you
feel mad with me just tell me to lay off and I will.' She
picked up another sandwich and looked at it steadily
as she continued, 'Where have you met our boss
before?'

Melanie started and the coffee in her beaker spilled
over the side on to her skirt.

'I – we haven't—'

'Before you get yourself all tied up in knots, I'd like
to remind you of something. A couple of days ago
when we were out there cleaning the verandah you
referred to him as Lean.' Her blue eyes were on Melanie, fixing hers in an interrogating stare.

'I did?' She had not noticed, but it could easily have
happened, for Melanie could not think of her former
fiancé as Mr. Angeli. Always in her thoughts he was

Lean. 'So you've guessed we're not strangers.'

'Obviously you're not strangers — and obviously there's a mystery. Feel like confiding in little old Auntie Sandra?'

In spite of herself a smile touched the corners of Melanie's mouth. Sandra was a tonic; she was going to make life bearable for the time she would be here, and after a moment's hesitation Melanie told her exactly what had happened.

As her narrative was unfolded Sandra's expression changed several times, but the only interruption she made was at the beginning when Melanie calmly told her of the jilting.

'You could have married him! You could have had *him*? You must have been crazy! I'd swoon if he only gave me a smile!'

'You would?' Melanie examined her friend's face with a mingling of wonderment and disbelief. 'But you said he was like Olga, said he could make you feel like a worm.'

'True ... but he could also make you feel like a queen.'

Melanie thought about that, frowningly as, against her will, she brought back the memory of Lean's kisses, blushing at the secret admission that they had thrilled and excited her in a way she had never experienced either before or since. Casting away these embarrassing and strangely disturbing reflections, she proceeded with her story and Sandra listened in silence until she had finished.

Strangely, Sandra was not as surprised by the story as Melanie expected her to be, for, having lived for several months in Greece, she had learned something of the Greek character. The Cretans, she had discovered since coming to the island, were even more vindictive than the metropolitan Greeks when it came to the avenging of a slight.

'I can quite see Lean Angeli harbouring a desire for revenge,' she said thoughtfully, pouring herself coffee from the flask they had brought out with them. 'So much is explained now – that awful room. What a diabolical thing, to put you in there! He could at least have given you a bit of comfort. But he's obviously intending to make you feel you're in prison.' Melanie made no comment and Sandra went on, 'So that's why Olga's as she is with you.'

'Olga?' Melanie spoke the word absently, for a late Etesian wind sent the oleander bushes swaying so that the perfume of the flowers filled the air. Melanie revelled in it, at the same time marvelling at the way the light, with its peculiar quality of radiance and clarity, gave to every object a sharpness of edge and outline. Truly there was something vastly different about the light of Greece; it was a perpetual source of wonder to Melanie, a sort of revelation.

'Everyone's noticing how she picks on you, even Kyrios. And the Greek women are gossiping about it. Things like this puzzle them, you both being English and yet not getting along.'

A flush mounted Melanie's cheeks as she brought her gaze from the oleanders and stared at her friend. It was true, Olga Newson did take every opportunity of finding fault with her work, and Melanie suspected she was being reported daily to her employer. But apart from that first occasion he had never sent for her. In fact, Melanie had not set eyes on him for the past three days.

'As I said, we made a bad start.'

'Of course. . . .' Sandra paused in thought. 'She must be seething at not being able to get you the sack.' A low chuckle left her lips. 'The boss will never sack you, whatever you do, and she must be wondering why

34

her complaints aren't bearing fruit.' Sandra gave a crow of delight. 'That's why she's always at you!'

Indignation shone in Melanie's eyes.

'There's no need for you to be so happy about it!'

'I didn't mean it like that,' Sandra glanced apologetically at her. 'It's the idea of Olga's being beaten that I'm so glad about.'

A tiny frown appeared between Melanie's eyes.

'Would – Mr. Angeli dismiss one of his staff simply because Olga took a dislike to her?'

'No, not just for that. But as you've noticed, he doesn't concern himself much with us – in fact he's away from the island for part of his time – and Olga is virtually in charge of the staff. On two occasions she's taken a dislike to one of the maids and they've had to go. She can concoct up anything,' Sandra added, shrugging. 'I expect she says they're lazy or something, and he'll take her word for it.'

'Then he shouldn't,' Melanie returned indignantly. 'That's very lax of him.'

'I don't know. . . . What hotel owner – especially one in a big way like Lean Angeli – would concern himself with the staff? It would be beneath his dignity.'

For some reason Melanie felt a tinge of bitterness on hearing that. Beneath his dignity to concern himself with her – for she was one of his staff. And to think that he had once desired her for his wife! Her glance strayed to Sandra, and she thought of what she had said a few moments ago. 'I'd swoon if he only gave me a smile!'

Melanie frowned, aware of a strange tingling of unrest as the vision of Lean Angeli rose up before her eyes, despite the determined effort to switch her thoughts. So different he was from the boy she had known. The years had enriched his personality with an added gravity and wisdom. Would this change have still occurred if she had married him? So remote and withdrawn he was, possessing all the majesty and aloofness of the gods themselves. It seemed impossible that he had ever loved her, that she could, had she wished, have had him for her husband.

'We'd better make a move.' Sandra began putting the flask and plates into the basket, and mechanically Melanie helped her. 'Otherwise we'll be hearing from our friend. She's just taking a look at us through the dining-room window.'

With a deep sigh Melanie left her pleasant and comfortable position under the shade of the carob tree and, picking up the basket, made for the back entrance of the hotel. A grand building it was, its attractive blue shutters contrasting with the walls whose whiteness was made more vivid by the exceptional brilliance of the light. Away behind rose the hills, and beyond those the central massif of limestone and schist, dominated by its snow-capped peaks, the highest of which was Mount Ida of the Ancients.

'It's lovely here. I wish I could get about more.'

'That's another thing,' returned Sandra almost angrily. 'To give you only Sunday off! I couldn't believe it when you told me what your working hours were. I wouldn't work those hours myself, since I don't see the point of being on an island like this and not being able to discover it. Why, you've seen nothing yet except the harbour and the square! And you're not likely to, unless you make a stand and demand more time off.'

'That will only prolong my stay,' Melanie said. 'For my wages wouldn't be as high.'

'What does he pay you?' asked Sandra after a small moment of hesitancy. 'You should be earning a bomb, the hours you put in.' When Melanie told her what she earned Sandra stopped dead in her tracks. 'Is that all he pays you?' she gasped unbelievingly, and Melanie nodded, a frown touching her forehead.

'How much do you receive?'

'Just double what you do. Melanie, this is robbery! You must do something about it. Look at the difference in hours. I finish every day at four, and I've all day Wednesday off, in addition to Sunday.' Her pretty face was flushed with anger and indignation. 'I wouldn't have it, Melanie. Go and see him and come to some different arrangement.'

'He said I was being paid the rate for the job,' Melanie told her as they started on their way again.

'That's the rate these peasant women usually get – but Mr. Angeli always pays a lot more – that I will give him, he's generous with his staff.'

'All except me,' Melanie reminded her bitterly. 'How can I ask for more if I'm receiving the recognised rate?'

'Tell him you know what I'm getting. I don't mind. You must try, Melanie, for as things are you'll never get the debt paid off.'

'That's just it. L— Mr. Angeli's determined to make the punishment last just as long as he's able.' She appeared resigned and Sandra pressed her again to take the matter of wages and hours up with Lean.

'Make an appointment with Olga, and get the matter cleared up so that you know just where you are. You can't go on like—' She stopped abruptly and then whispered, 'Just look at her face. She hates you, Melanie!'

Startled, Melanie shot a glance towards the dining-room window. Olga had disappeared.

'That's rather strong, isn't it? She dislikes me, but I see no reason why she should actually hate me.'

'No?' Sandra's blue eyes glinted perceptively. 'She must be racking her brains to know why her complaints are having no effect – for you can be sure she is complaining – and I'm warning you, Melanie, that woman can be poison. If she decided to get rid of you she'd go to any lengths to achieve her object.'

A shrug from Melanie, and then,

'She can't get rid of me, though, no matter what lengths to which she might go.'

'But she doesn't know that.' Sandra looked significantly at her. 'She's puzzled by what's going on, but is quite unaware that you won't ever be sacked. Watch her, Melanie, for it's my guess that she'll think up some way of blackening you in Mr. Angeli's eyes.'

'I think you're exaggerating,' Melanie began, when her friend interrupted her.

'I know her – have seen her with those two others.' Sandra paused before continuing in stressed, deliberate tones, 'Keep it in your mind that she doesn't know you'll never lose your job ... and act accordingly. By that I mean – take care!'

CHAPTER THREE

'ALL this jewellery!' exclaimed Sandra, as she and Melanie were working together, making one of the beds. 'Even under the pillow! Earrings, and they're real diamonds too. I hate it when people leave such things about. Look at that dressing-table. Where do these people get their money?'

'Americans always seem to be rich,' commented Melanie without so much as a glance at the earrings which her friend held up in order to examine admiringly. 'This Mrs. Skonson must be the wife of a millionaire, judging by the lovely things she has.'

'Do you think she'd miss these?' Sandra grinned, dropping them into her apron pocket.

'Probably not,' responded Melanie, laughing at the gesture. 'How much can you sell them for?'

'Probably a thousand.' Sandra withdrew them again and put them on the dressing-table. 'I haven't a clue about things like that, never having owned anything more valuable than the glass variety.'

'A thousand,' murmured Melanie absently, speaking her thoughts aloud, for that particular amount was indelibly imprinted on her mind. 'Just enough to clear my debt.'

Both girls glanced up, to see Olga standing in the doorway, watching them with a curious expression in her eyes.

'What are you doing, working together?' she demanded sharply. 'Melanie, why aren't you in your own area?'

'It's easier, and more pleasant, working together,' Sandra put in quickly. 'The work gets done just the same—'

'You'll each do your own!' Olga snapped, her eyes flicking from Melanie to the dressing-table and back again. 'Get to your own rooms, and don't let me find you wandering in this part of the corridor again!'

'Wandering?' echoed Melanie, treating her to a stare as haughty as her own. 'I don't think I understand you.'

'This is not your area! Get back at once!'

Sandra cast Melanie a glance of warning, and although she was now white with fury and quite ready to do battle with this detestable woman, that glance of Sandra's had an odd effect on her. For some reason she experienced a pang of fear and, obeying an inner warning that seemed to supplement that just silently conveyed to her by Sandra, Melanie came from the far side of the bed and, as Sandra stepped out of the way to let her pass, she left the room without another word.

A short while later, on glancing through the window of the bedroom she was cleaning, Melanie saw Lean and Olga in the garden below. They were sitting in deck chairs by the clear, palm-shaded swimming-pool, Lean in white linen slacks and shirt and Olga in a brief sun-dress revealing the tan of her thighs and her elegant shoulders. Beautiful, but a viper, Sandra had said when, yesterday, she and Melanie had looked down on a similar scene. On that occasion Olga had an account book on her lap; today she and Lean were deep in conversation.

As Melanie watched, a white-coated waiter brought out refreshments and placed them on a small table which he then carried over and put before Lean and Olga. They were having coffee; Olga poured it out, then handed Lean his cup, which he took from her, smiling as he did so. The smile transformed his face, veiling the hardness, the flint-like impassivity, and bringing to his features an attractiveness that stirred her memory fleetingly as she strove to grasp a vision rather in the manner one tries to catch and hold a chord of some sweet elusive melody. Restlessness pervaded her and she turned away, an unaccountable frown appearing to mar the beauty of her clear wide brow. But almost immediately it disappeared, for Sandra came in, carrying two glasses of lemonade.

'They're both outside in the garden, so we're safe,' she grinned, sitting on the bed and holding out one of the glasses to her friend. 'I'm going to sneak off now and cook us a meal. You're invited to lunch in my room. All right?'

A swift smile spread as Melanie thanked her.

'That will be nice,' she added, and then, 'You're not afraid of Olga's missing you?'

'They look as if they'll be out there for ages, so I'm chancing it. Come up as soon as you've finished.'

'I will.' Melanie sat down on a chair to drink her lemonade. 'This is good. Thanks for bringing it to me. I was just beginning to wonder how I'd manage till lunch time.' Unconsciously her eyes strayed to the window. Sandra watched her musingly and then, rising from the bed, she strolled over and glanced down to the garden.

'They're having coffee,' she remarked in an expressionless tone. 'Did you see them a few moments ago? She was practically on his lap.'

'The coffee was just being brought when I looked out.' Melanie drained her glass and stood up, but she remained at the other side of the room.

'Don't you feel anything when you see them together?' Sandra turned as she asked the question and looked curiously at her friend.

'This is the first time I've seen them together. No, I don't feel anything.'

41

'Gosh, I would! I couldn't bear it.' Her gaze became searching. 'I don't know how you could give him up. You said the engagement was just a – well, a lark on your part – but you must have felt something for him.'

Absently Melanie toyed with the empty glass in her hand.

'He was . . . different,' she murmured evasively.

'Not at all. The same man, but younger. How old was he?'

'Twenty-four.'

'And it's seven years ago, you said? He wasn't terribly young,' she added thoughtfully. 'Old enough to know his own mind, evidently.'

A smile curved Melanie's lips; it gave a hint of bitterness of which she herself was totally unaware.

'The same age as I am now.'

Sandra held out her hand for Melanie's empty glass.

'And you would, at this age, know your own mind?'

'I'd not accept a man's ring unless I intended marrying him.'

'And so you can appreciate his feelings at that time?'

Melanie nodded.

'Yes, I can.' Although she answered instantly there was that in her tone which indicated a reluctance to continue the conversation and Sandra changed the subject.

'It's an English lunch I'm cooking. How do you like your steak?'

'Medium, please.'

'Same as me. See you later.'

The door closed behind her and Melanie walked over to the window again. Still there, in earnest conversation. . . .

Half an hour later Melanie looked out once more, this time from the window of another bedroom. The garden was occupied only by the tourists, Americans, mostly, for a party had come in a couple of days ago and were staying about a week. Glancing at her watch Melanie saw that it was five minutes to one, and after only a slight hesitation she made up her mind. Lean would be in his office; she felt she must have a word with him over the question of her hours and pay, especially as Sandra had said earlier that morning that she was going to Knossos on the following Wednesday, and had expressed regret that Melanie could not accompany her.

A long delay followed her knock on Lean's door, but at length Melanie was invited to enter. To her consternation Olga was there, her flushed face causing Melanie's glance to pass covertly from her to Lean. Had they been in one another's arms?

'Yes?' The smile instantly faded from Lean's face and the arrogant brows lifted as he saw who it was. 'What do you want?'

Conscious of the other girl's hostile stare, Melanie found herself stammering.

'I'd l-like to speak to-to you privately—'

'Appointments to see me are made through Miss Newson,' he snapped, cutting her short. 'See her later and she'll arrange a time.'

'Yes.' Melanie looked at Olga. 'You'll be in your office all the afternoon?'

Lean was watching Olga and to Melanie's utter astonishment the older girl bestowed on her a most pleasant and friendly smile.

'Until about five,' she returned affably. 'Come any time before then.'

'Thank you.' Keeping her head lowered, Melanie

43

went out and up to Sandra's room on the second floor.

'You look hot and bothered,' her friend commented. 'Take a seat.'

'I went to see Lean about my hours and salary,' she said, walking over to the window. It was wide open and led on to a balcony from where could be seen a view of the town. 'He made me feel like a worm, just as you once remarked.'

'Made you—?' Sandra paused on her way into the tiny kitchen leading off the spacious and airy bed-sitting room. 'What happened? Didn't you get anything sorted out?'

'I chose a bad time; Olga was there. Lean snapped at me and told me to make an appointment through her.'

Sandra nodded.

'That's right, you have to. The boss won't see you otherwise. I thought you knew.'

'I did have an idea,' admitted Melanie, 'but I acted on impulse. It was five to one and I thought it would be a good time to speak to him for a few minutes.'

Sandra grinned.

'Expected preferential treatment—'

'No, of course not,' came the swift interruption. 'But I simply hate the idea of having to go to that girl first.'

'You're going to, though?'

'Yes.' Melanie turned into the room. 'Olga was all honey, as you might say. It's obvious that Lean doesn't know how she treats his staff.'

'Honey, was she?' Sandra stood in the doorway and stared questioningly at her friend. 'To you, you mean?'

'She was quite different, friendly and pleasant.'

A half sneer was Sandra's response as she went into

44

the kitchen, returning a moment or two later with a dish of vegetables which she placed on the table. It was set to one side of the window and looked pretty and inviting with its snow-white cloth and flowers and wine.

'Pleasant,' Sandra repeated musingly. 'Yes, you're right; the boss will be completely in the dark as to how we're treated. I don't come into contact with her all that much. For some reason she hasn't bothered me. In any case, I've only a few months left – not like you, having to stay all that time.'

'I wish I could find some way out of this mess!' Melanie exclaimed, feeling life would be completely unbearable once Sandra had left the hotel, and the island.

'I know how you feel.' Sandra went into the kitchen for the meat. 'You'll be a nervous wreck long before you've cleared yourself of that debt.' She returned, put the meat on the table, and sniffed. 'Hmm. .... Help yourself to the bathroom and then let's have a good tuck in.'

The bathroom also led off the main room. It was light and high, with both bath and shower. It was all white and chrome, and had a long mirror on one wall. Sandra's toilet things were laid about daintily, and a flowering plant stood on a glass shelf at the foot of the bath. Melanie washed her hands and returned to the other room. She had earlier taken a look in at the room just along the corridor. It was similar to this, with rugs and comfortable furniture and, as Sandra had remarked, the view was even superior to hers.

'Sandra,' said Melanie as they sat eating their lunch, 'do you know of any way I could supplement my money?'

'I thought you were going to tackle the boss?'

'I am, but he'll not give me any extra. And even if he

45

did,' she added. 'I'd still like to earn some more.'

'In one day?' Sandra shook her head. 'What could you do? Besides, you'd knock yourself up.'

'These people – the women, that is – work seven days.'

'They rest, though. They're always getting down and having a sleep. No, Melanie, you can't do anything.' She pushed the vegetables over to her. 'Have some more.'

'Thanks.' Melanie picked up the spoon. 'Wouldn't anyone employ me for Sundays? What about the shops – don't they want English speaking people to serve?'

'The Greeks speak English – enough to get by with the tourists.' She paused and her eyes flickered. 'You're quite serious?' she asked at length.

'Yes.' Forgetting all about the extra helping of vegetables, Melanie stared at her friend with an expression of eager expectancy. 'You've thought of something?'

'A young Englishman I've met ... he's on the wander, too, and out to make what he can. He has one or two wealthy Cretan clients to whom he teaches English— No, that's not right. They speak English fairly well, and all he does is to sit with them for a few hours a week and they talk together.' ·

'You can make money in this way?' Melanie trembled with excitement. Only to sit. . . . That would not tire her at all. 'How much?'

'He gets well paid – a pound an hour, I think he said. This happens everywhere, now I come to think of it. Any reasonably well-educated English person can earn money like this. Now,' she added, knitting her brows, 'we'll have to make a date to see him. Leave it to me,' she went on decisively. 'I'll see him one evening this week, and find out if he can help you. You're not going to see anything of the island, though, not if you work on Sundays.'

'I've given up hope of that anyway. You can't get about on nothing.'

'He isn't giving you a single penny?'

'Not a penny.'

'But – my God, in gaol you get something! What about the necessities like soap and toothpaste and the rest?'

'I brought my savings with me – but I've made up my mind not to spend one shilling more than I need. I'm getting out of this place just as soon as I possibly can.'

'I don't blame you. You can always come back some day and have a holiday. . . .' Sandra tailed off and gave a little selfconscious laugh. 'Stupid me! You'll never want to set foot on the shores of Crete again!'

'I'll never set foot on the shores of Greece again!' was Melanie's fervent response as at last she helped herself to the vegetables. 'And as for the people, I never want to meet any of them again either!'

But Melanie changed her opinion of the Cretans on meeting Kostagis and his wife Androula, the charming young couple to whom Giles Turner introduced her the following evening. By accident Sandra had run into Giles within a few hours of her promising to contact him; he had immediately offered to take Melanie to see some people desirous of improving their English, but whom he himself could not help as he had all the clients he could manage.

'You like Crete?' asked Kostagis after the introductions had been made and they were all sitting out on the verandah, enjoying the cool of the evening. It was dark, but with a moon which shone over the sea and a million stars twinkling from a sky of deepest purple. Cicadas were chirping in the trees, and from the mountains, blending indistinctly with the sky and clouds, came a welcome breeze, scented with an exotic fragrance picked up on its way through the gentle wooded foothills.

'I – yes, I like what I've seen,' Melanie replied awkwardly. 'I've not been on the island very long, so can't really pass an opinion.'

'No?' Androula tilted her pretty dark head to one side in a rather enchanting gesture she had when something puzzled her. 'But always everyone like the Kriti. No peoples say not pass – pass opinion.'

'What Melanie means,' said Giles slowly, 'is that she hasn't seen your beautiful island yet, so she doesn't know if she likes it or not.'

'Not like?' Androula frowned, but before she could continue her husband interrupted.

'Melanie does like our island. But she like it better if we take her round. Yes?' Still some puzzlement on his wife's face so Kostagis explained in their own language. A bright smile appeared on Androula's face and she laughed delightedly.

'We take in car – to see all Kriti.'

'There you are.' Giles spread his hands. 'The typical Cretan hospitality. They'll give you a marvellous time, and take you everywhere. Don't be afraid to ask.'

'No, not afraid to ask.' It was clear that Kostagis spoke English much better than his wife and it was arranged that Melanie should spend two hours on Sunday morning with them both, and an hour on Mondays and Wednesdays with Androula on her own. Kostagis went out those nights, out to the café to forget his wife and his marriage for a few hours as he, along with many of his friends, went back to the days of their freedom. This was quite normal; with Kostagis it was for two nights only, but with the majority of Greeks the companionship of marriage lasted one year at most, and from then on they would be found with their friends, sprawling in some pavement café, reading the

48

newspaper or playing cards, while their wives would gather in one or another of the houses, or in some vine-shaded courtyard, chatting together while their fingers, gradually becoming gnarled and almost black from their work in the fields, would work industriously at the beautiful embroidery for which Greek women were famed.

'You have told Melanie what we are willing to pay?' Kostagis asked the question of Giles and Sandra threw Melanie a quick expectant glance.

'You'll pay a pound an hour? That's normal, Kostagis.'

'Yes, yes. I not argue. We want to learn English and we pay.'

'On Sundays it will be double, because there are two of you.' Obviously Giles was used to this. Melanie would not have dreamed of charging double. However because of her desperation to earn as much as possible she refrained from interrupting, allowing Giles to get for her the best deal possible.

'Sundays two pounds an hour,' agreed Kostagis amicably. 'And now, my friends, let me take you all to nice hotel I know, and we have some drinks and a *meze*.'

'Six pounds a week!' Melanie exclaimed three hours later when she and Sandra arrived back at the Hotel Avra. 'How marvellous! I couldn't believe it. I do hope I thanked Giles enough. And you, Sandra . . . I'm ever so grateful. I feel so much better already at the thought of being able to reduce this debt.'

They were in Sandra's room, having the coffee she had made. It was after twelve, but Melanie felt as fresh as if she had just risen from her bed. A great weight had suddenly been lifted from her shoulders. Four years of purgatory . . . ? Lean Angeli had a shock coming to him.

'How will you do it?' inquired Sandra curiously, her

pretty, rather chubby face creased in thought. 'Will you save it up and pay it off every month, or what?'

Melanie shook her head.

'I'll save it, certainly, but until I've enough to clear the debt. And then—' She broke off, her lovely eyes sparkling with anticipation. 'Then I'll present this balance to Lean and bid him a glad goodbye!'

Sandra laughed at that, but almost instantly became serious.

'Whatever you do, don't forget Giles's warning. Foreigners can't earn money in these countries without work permits. I don't know what our boss does, but in any case he's a big pull, because he must be the richest man on the island. He has a fortune in carob plantations, and as you probably know he owns hotels all over Greece. So no one is going to worry him or refuse his requests for permits for his staff. But with anyone like you and Giles, doing work on the side, so to speak, you have to be very secretive. Giles, as you heard, explained to Kostagis, and Kostagis will naturally co-operate. But, for heaven's sake, never breathe a word about this other employment you're engaged in.'

'I'll be very careful. Giles said that if ever I'm questioned I must say Kostagis and Androula are my friends and that I'm merely visiting them socially.'

'That's what he does. And somehow his clients pay him in English pounds because he wants to take the money out of the country when the urge strikes him again, but you'll be paid in drachmae.' A thoughtful silence and then Sandra went on to ask how Melanie meant to save her money. 'Will you put it in the bank?'

'No, I'd be afraid of questions. Supposing the bank manager happened to know Lean?'

'That's possible. And if he did then you can be sure he'd talk. You'll hide your money away somewhere,

50

then?'

'In my room. There are plenty of places,' she added with a hint of bitterness. 'Under the floor, for one. All the flagstones are loose.'

Sandra frowned and said she'd get ants.

'Dozens of them,' Melanie replied, shuddering at the memory of stepping out of bed that first morning and putting her foot on what to her horrified imagination was a whole nest of ants.

'You seem to have made a hit with Giles,' remarked Sandra, changing the subject. 'But watch him; he's a flirt.'

'I've already gathered that,' Melanie laughed. 'He's nice, though.'

'I'm glad I took you to meet him; perhaps your life will be a little more pleasant now. Wasn't it nice of Kostagis to suggest taking you around?' Melanie nodded, but went on to say that she could scarcely take advantage of his offer with having so little time available.

'Besides,' she added, 'I couldn't go out with them and not pay my way; I'd feel too uncomfortable.'

'You'd have no need to,' Sandra assured her, 'because they're really sincere in their offer. The Greeks are all like that – offering you hospitality. There just aren't any people in the world like them – even the peasants would give you their last.' She shook her head emphatically. 'No, Melanie, you mustn't trouble yourself about that. And as for having no time, I thought you said you'd make an appointment to see the boss about that.'

'I have; the appointment's for ten in the morning.'

'Talking about the morning,' grinned Sandra with a glance at the clock, 'we'd better be making a move, otherwise we'll never be up.' She paused, eyeing the couch. 'You can kip down here if you want to, Melanie. That couch is ever so comfortable.'

But Melanie shook her head.

'It's kind of you,' she returned gratefully. 'But I'm used to that place now. It's just a matter of getting into bed and getting out again. I don't even look at my surroundings.'

'Well, don't forget what I said – you can share this place with me for the rest of the time, and even if I'm out you can use it. And you mustn't even think of using that horrid old bathroom again. Bring your stuff down here; I'll clear out one side of the cabinet for you, and I know where there's a towel rail I can pinch – there are three in one of the guest rooms, so no one'll miss it. You'll feel better, more at home if you have your own separate things.'

'You're so kind, Sandra.' Melanie had difficulty in finding words, but eventually she managed to add, 'Life would have been quite unbearable if I hadn't met you.'

'Nonsense—'

'It's true.'

'Oh, well, aren't we all here to help one another? Come,' she continued briskly, 'we've only five hours – and I'm not good at getting up at the best of times!'

Promptly at ten the following morning Melanie presented herself at Lean's office.

'It's about my hours,' she submitted, standing by his desk, her hands clasped in front of her. 'They're too long.'

The icy glance of her former fiancé sent a shiver through her. How very disconcerting he was!

'Where's your uniform?'

Melanie's delicate skin changed from ivory to peach and then to crimson as the blood rushed to her cheeks.

52

'Uniform?' she repeated quiveringly.

'The room maids wear aprons and bands to keep back their hair.' His gaze remained on her hair for a moment and automatically Melanie flicked it away from her face. It fell on to her shoulders, honey-gold and shining. Lean – the Lean she had known – had loved to bury his face in her hair, murmuring about its softness and its colour.

'I took them off to come here.'

'What do you want?' His tones were low and clipped, his manner one of bored impatience.

'It's about my hours,' she said again, fully aware that he was deliberately making her repeat her words. 'I – I think they should be shorter, and – and I would like another day off.'

'What are your hours?'

He knew, of course, but Melanie said patiently,

'From six till eight.' He said nothing and she added, 'That's fourteen hours a day.'

'You have a lunch break, I presume?' he questioned with a lift of his brow.

'An hour, yes.'

'And breaks morning and afternoon?'

'Half an hour – I mean, an hour in all.'

'So you work twelve hours, not fourteen as you've just stated.'

'Yes,' she admitted, 'it is twelve hours I work.'

Lean's brows lifted a fraction higher.

'Then why did you tell me it was fourteen? Are you a liar as well as a thief?'

Her colour heightened again, a circumstance that afforded Lean some satisfaction, judging by the expression on his face, and Melanie lowered her head. Why this reluctance to flare up? – to show him her spirit?

'Twelve is still too many hours,' she said, recovering

53

her composure 'And with having only one day off – I've to do my own jobs, and then most of the day's gone.'

'Already you're complaining?' His eyes held hers for a moment before moving over her, taking in every detail, she felt, frowning inwardly as an unaccountable embarrassment threatened to bring a return of the colour to her cheeks. 'You do realize that were I to shorten your hours your money would naturally be cut?'

She did flare then, telling him he was not paying her enough as it was, and that even if her hours were shortened she wanted more pay.

'You're receiving the rate for the job,' he told her quietly, leaning right back in his chair as if to regard her from a greater distance.

'The rate for these Greek women!' The words had escaped before she realized her phrasing was wrong and her heart actually fluttered even before he spoke.

'You consider yourself above them?' His accent became pronounced as he added in slow-and measured tones, 'Get your values straight, Melanie. They're good and honest women, the salt of the earth ... you and your like are the trash.'

She flinched. Trash. ... Once he had whispered, with an even more pronounced accent,

'My lovely *koré* – you surpass every other girl I have ever met.' And as memory brought back that vibrant declaration Melanie once again spoke without stopping to consider her words.

'I've changed, Lean. I'm not so stupid now; I was scatter-brained then, and thoughtless. You – you don't make allowances for my youth at that time.' She looked at him across the desk, her lovely eyes wide and re-pentant, and a little too bright. 'I wouldn't behave like that now – over – over the engagement, I mean.'

'Are you asking for mercy?' he inquired, not without a touch of humour. 'If so then you're wasting your time.'

'Not mercy,' she denied quickly, crushed by his amusement and the indifferent way in which he had dismissed her plea for understanding. 'But I do ask for justice, Lean—' His eyes were staring past her and Melanie turned. She had not closed the door properly on entering and it had softly opened on being pushed by Olga, who was standing there, a sheaf of papers in her hand.

'I'm so sorry, Lean,' she said with a ready smile. 'I thought you would be finished with Melanie by now. I'll come back later.' Her eyes flickered to Melanie . . . and in their dark depths there dwelt something that sent an involuntary shiver down her spine.

'Is it just signing?' he inquired with a glance at the papers in Olga's hand. 'If so, you can leave them.'

'There are a few queries, but nothing urgent. I'll bring them in later.' Another glance in Melanie's direction and then Olga was gone, the door catch clicking softly behind her. How much had she heard? wondered Melanie as she murmured apologetically,

'I shouldn't have called you Lean. It just slipped out.'

His attention appeared to be on the closed door and silence reigned for some moments before he brought his gaze back to Melanie. Either he had not heard her apology or he chose to ignore it as he said,

'What is this justice which you're requesting I extend to you?'

She moved restlessly; her face pale, her thoughts still on the girl who had just gone out.

'You pay Sandra much more than me, and she doesn't work these long hours.' A sudden frown betrayed his thoughts and Melanie hastily went on, 'Sandra said I could mention this – otherwise I wouldn't have dreamed of doing so.'

'You and Sandra have been comparing lots? Sandra is receiving much more than the recognized rate simply because I consider she is worth it. You, on the other hand, are worth no more than you're getting.'

Melanie had known what his answer would be, and she now bitterly regretted having come here, placing herself in this humiliating position.

'So I can't have the day off, either?'

'Certainly not.'

'The room,' she persevered. 'Must I remain in that? There's another room vacant—'

'A girl is coming into it next week. There's nowhere else for you to go, but even if there were,' he added deliberately, 'I wouldn't let you move. That room is part of the punishment and you'll remain in it until you leave here – in about four years' time.'

'Four years—!' Prudently Melanie pulled herself up. But she no longer made any effort to control her anger and she added quiveringly, 'What kind of a man are you? This form of punishment must be the worst you could possibly think up!'

'You believe so?' he queried calmly. 'No, Melanie, you're wrong; I could – did in fact – think up a worse punishment.' His dark eyes became embers of hate and the long lean fingers resting on the arm of the chair closed, slowly, in a sort of cruel relentless movement that made Melanie raise a hand involuntarily to her throat. 'I could have forced you to marry me.' The embers burned themselves out and the hand on the arm of the chair relaxed. 'Be thankful for your lot, Melanie,' he advised, 'for as your husband I'd have taught you a good deal more about punishment.'

Lean brought himself forward and became concerned with his appointment book. It was some moments before Melanie grasped the significance of his action, realized that it was in fact a dismissal. Silently she turned and left the room, more determined than ever to escape from this man's power just as quickly as she could.

CHAPTER FOUR

MRS. SKONSON had lost her earrings. They were worth seven hundred and fifty pounds, and she firmly maintained they had been stolen from the drawer in her dressing-table, where she distinctly remembered putting them on taking them off the previous night.

'It's rumoured that the boss has sent for the police.' Sandra and Melanie were in their usual spot in the garden, having a snack lunch of sandwiches and coffee. 'I have my doubts about that, though, for he wouldn't want that sort of publicity. Perhaps he'll investigate himself.'

'They can't have been stolen.' Melanie sat back in her deck chair enjoying the sunshine, and this precious hour during which she escaped from the drudgery of her work. It was Tuesday and she glanced with envy at her friend. Only another couple of hours' work this afternoon and then Sandra would be free until Thursday morning. 'None of the staff would touch them, and as she always locks her room none of the guests could do so. She must have lost them outside – and yet I can't imagine how.'

'Nor can I. One could fall off, but I can't see her losing both in this way.'

'I wonder how Lean will go about it – if he does decide to investigate himself.'

Sandra shrugged carelessly.

'In the same way as the police, I suppose. Question all the staff and if nothing comes of it he'll have all our rooms searched.'

'It's a most unsavoury business,' Melanie frowned,

her gaze on the scene on the opposite side of the road. Tall palms and pines shaded the café, and as usual men sprawled under them. Occasionally a peasant woman would pass, dressed entirely in black, leading a reluctant donkey, its back laden with fruit and vegetables. The atmosphere was hot and airless and the road surface shimmered in the heat.

'Bad for us all,' Sandra agreed. 'The trouble with Mrs. Skonson is that she just has too many of this world's goods.'

Melanie brought her gaze from the café and looked at her friend.

'Yes, I suppose we're all suspect.'

'But as you've just said, none of the staff would touch them. These Greek women would be scared at the very thought of stealing a single drachma, let alone a pair of diamond earrings. And that leaves only you and me.' Again she shrugged. 'So she must have lost them outside. Put them down in a wash place somewhere and left them on the basin. It wouldn't be the first time it's happened.'

The lunch hour was all too fleeting and it was soon time for them to return to their work. Five minutes after Melanie had begun cleaning out one of the vacant bedrooms Olga Newson came to her. What fault would she find this time? Melanie wondered, ready to hold her own at the first sign of complaint. But a break was suddenly put on her thoughts as she saw Olga's expression.

'Leave what you're doing and come with me!' Olga ordered, standing with the door in her hand waiting for Melanie to precede her.

'With you?' Melanie frowned at her questioningly. 'Where to?'

'Mr. Angeli wants to see you, at once!'

Melanie's frown deepened. There was something in

59

the nature of triumph in Olga's manner, and a strange expectancy.

The moment she saw Lean's face Melanie's heartbeats quickened, for there was a fury in his eyes she had never before encountered.

He came straight to the point. Indicating the earrings lying on his desk, he said in a voice vibrant with anger and contempt,

'These have been found in your room. What have you to say?'

Bereft of speech, Melanie could only stand there, on the opposite side of the desk, staring with a sort of fascinated wonderment at the diamonds gleaming there.

'Wh-what d-did you say?' she stammered at last.

Lean's eyes smouldered.

'Never before has such a thing occurred in one of my hotels! How did you expect to get away with it?'

Melanie's glance darted to Olga. The older girl was standing over by the window, that mingling of triumph and expectancy on her face as she silently looked on.

'Are you accusing me of stealing Mrs. Skonson's earrings?' Melanie's voice was barely audible. In spite of her innocence the colour slowly receded from her face.

'I'm saying you did steal them! Miss Newson found them hidden in the mattress of your bed.'

'Miss Newson found them ... in my mattress?' Dazed, yet with comprehension slowly dawning, she threw another glance at the girl of whom her friend had warned her to be careful. 'If you said you found them in my room,' she went on with difficulty, 'then you're lying, and you know it.'

Carelessly Olga shrugged, at the same time sending a significant glance in Lean's direction.

'Just as I expected, Lean. I told you she'd deny it.'

He then spoke almost as harshly to Olga as he had to Melanie.

'Leave us, please!'

'Certainly.'

Immediately the door closed Lean stood up and came round to Melanie's side of the desk.

'Are you denying you stole these earrings?'

'I never touched them.' She betrayed neither anger nor indignation, for her mind was completely bemused by the revelation that had come to her a moment ago as she looked into Olga Newson's eyes. 'They were never found in my room.'

'Miss Newson is a liar?' A scornful glance accompanied his words.

'I've just said so, and I meant it.' She was white to the lips, but a strange dignity entered into her, and although Lean was far too close for comfort she looked up to meet his gaze unflinchingly. 'Why should I want to steal Mrs. Skonson's earrings? They're no good to me.'

A small silence ensued. Vaguely Melanie was aware of the chirp of cicadas from the direction of the open window, and the heady and exotic fragrance of oleanders.

'Is it true that Miss Newson found you in Mrs. Skonson's bedroom?'

'Sandra and I were working together, and—'

'Answer my question!'

'Yes, but—'

'Is it also true that she overheard you and Sandra discussing the probable price for which these earrings could be sold?'

'I – we were joking about it – you see, Mrs. Skonson left the earrings under her pillow and Sandra found them. . . .' Melanie tailed off, suddenly engulfed in a feeling of helplessness. She had truth on her side, but she was not convincing him of her innocence. With a sort of desperation in her eyes she waited for him to speak, almost willing him not to condemn her out of hand, even while admitting that he could not be blamed for doing so.

'Miss Newson heard you say the words "Just enough to clear my debt". She didn't understand the meaning of that, because she's in ignorance of the reason for your coming here, but I understand, don't I?'

Trembling from head to foot, Melanie strove to frame an explanation that would impress itself upon him, but she failed.

'Sandra said they'd probably be worth a thousand pounds,' she faltered. 'That sum had – had become an obsession with me, and I said that about the debt, but it was a sort of automatic reaction to Sandra's guessing at the worth of the earrings. I didn't mean it seriously. You must believe me?'

He didn't believe her, that was plain from his derisive glance. But there was something else about him too, something about him she could not fathom – a strange tenseness and a sort of . . . bitterness.

'They were found in your room,' he reminded her quietly. 'You're the only one who could have put them there.' She merely shook her head despairingly and he went on, in a voice tinged with accusation, 'You said yourself you intended supplementing your wages so that the debt could be paid. You might just as well own up, for I know from your former behaviour that you're a thief. I think you'll agree that there's nothing to be gained by these denials.'

Defeated, but retaining her dignity, Melanie said that although appearances were against her, that so many incidents occurring recently pointed to her guilt, she was not a thief.

'Some day the truth might come out,' she added

miserably. 'I don't know. For the present, you believe I took the earrings, and I can't convince you otherwise – but for me, my conscience is clear. I didn't touch them and therefore I couldn't have put them in my mattress.' And she added, as though the thought occurred to her, 'Have any of the other rooms been searched?'

'Yours was the last to be searched.'

'Miss Newson told you this?'

'I have no reason to disbelieve her,' he snapped.

'Did anyone help her with the searching of these rooms?'

'You're insinuating that no other rooms were searched?'

'I'm *saying* that no rooms at all were searched.' She looked at him with a wide and honest gaze, but he seemed not to notice. 'You have only Miss Newson's word that the rooms were searched—'

'Her word's good enough for me.' More reliable than yours, his glance said clearly, and Melanie was left wondering why he had not spoken those words aloud.

With a helpless, defeated little gesture she spread her hands.

'What are you going to do?'

'Do?' He frowned at her absently and she realized to her amazement that he had little grey lines at the corners of his mouth as if he were rather tired or dispirited. 'Nothing. Fortunately the matter has been dealt with without my having to call in the police. You'll be carefully watched in future, but I think that even you will be wise enough not to try this sort of thing again.'

The 'even you' spoke volumes. Melanie's lips trembled as she asked, huskily, if there was anything else he wanted to say.

'You're not in the least contrite, are you?' Contempt

in his tones, but Melanie frowned. For there was no mistaking the edge of bitterness to his voice. 'You're thoroughly shameless,' he added, and waved a hand towards the door. 'No, I've nothing else to say to you. You may go.'

She instantly went in search of Olga, but she was nowhere to be found. After making inquiries of practically every one of the staff, Melanie at last learned from Kyrios that Olga had gone off to Knossos with a party of guests from the hotel.

Although scarcely able to contain her fury, Melanie had no alternative than to await Olga's return. But, unable to work, she went up to her friend's room and told her what had taken place. Sandra's blue eyes opened very wide, but after a few moments of thoughtful silence she was less surprised than Melanie expected.

'She's jealous,' asserted Sandra. 'I knew from the first there was something, for she was always at you – and I should have known it was jealousy because she used to be jealous of Wendy, the girl whom I spoke to you about, the one who went off to the Holy Land. Wendy was really pretty and the boss was fond of her – he didn't flirt with her or anything like that,' added Sandra hastily, 'but they got on together and often would sit chatting in the garden. Olga would be seething and the following day she'd start on poor Wendy again, finding fault with her work. But she was never as bad with her as she's been with you.' She paused, smiling at her friend's expression. 'It's true, so you needn't look like that; Olga's definitely jealous of you. As I said before, she's been puzzled because her complaints to the boss haven't born fruit – and also, Melanie, you've been rather careless about calling your ex-fiancé Lean in her hearing.'

'Yes ... when we were talking about the earrings, but how did I know she was listening at the door?'

'That was not the only time. I didn't mention it to you, but on the first occasion when you let his name slip out before me she was on the balcony just above us. She must have heard, and naturally concluded that you had known Lean before coming here. Probably she'd wonder if you'd had an affair – I don't think for one moment she's suspected the truth, but you can bet your life she's been worrying herself sick—'

'Why should she?' Melanie couldn't help interrupting. 'Lean never even speaks to me.'

'Does she know that?'

'Perhaps not, but she knows what hours he makes me work, and she also knows what room I'm in.' Melanie shook her head. 'No, Sandra, she couldn't possibly be jealous of me or be worrying herself sick, as you put it.'

Sandra thought about this and then went on to give Melanie a few facts about Olga's character as she knew them.

'She has some peculiar traits,' said Sandra musingly. 'I feel she's had an unfortunate love affair at some time in her life and that it's left her feeling – in spite of her apparent confidence in her own attractions – a little afraid that someone might pinch Lean from her. For she can even be funny with a guest if the boss happens to show her a bit of attention. You're rather above the run beauty-wise—'

'Sandra, I'm not – please—'

'Very much above, so she's scared.'

'But I've just said that she knows the hours I work. It's so obvious that Lean doesn't like me.'

'All the more reason for Olga's being worried.'

'I don't know what you mean?'

'There's obviously been something between you previously – she knows this. Now, the boss appears to dislike you, but he could suddenly see you in a different light, fall in love with you and forget the past—'

'Lean would never fall in love with me!' Melanie was trembling and to her consternation the colour swiftly rose to her cheeks. 'The idea's ridiculous!'

'Of course it is, because you had a real bust-up, but Olga doesn't know this. She might be thinking you merely had a tiff and that Lean will forget it one of these days and there'll be a grand reunion. She must be afraid,' Sandra went on reasonably, 'to go to the lengths of making you out a thief.' She stopped, looking at Melanie with an odd expression as a thought occurred to her. 'You're going to tackle her, you say?'

'That's right, but she's gone off to Knossos with the guests.'

'Olga doesn't usually accompany the guests on tours. Don't you see, she's keeping out of the way for a few hours ... believing you'll be gone by the time she returns.'

'Gone?'

'Sacked – on the spot. Instant dismissal! She'd never have done a trick like that had she known she would have to face you. And what's she going to say when she discovers her scheme has failed?'

'My life's going to be more uncomfortable than ever.'

'I warned you to be careful – and I'm warning you again. She'll try something else – or my name's not Sandra!'

The moment the party returned, Melanie sought out Olga in her office.

'Come in,' called Olga in response to her knock, and Melanie quietly opened the door and stood just inside the room. 'You—!' Olga half rose from her chair and then sat down again. 'Wh-why haven't you g-gone? I take it you were instantly dismissed?'

So Sandra had been right in her assumption that Olga had gone with the guests purposely to avoid confrontation with Melanie.

'I'd like a few words with you.' Slowly Melanie advanced into the room, having pushed the door to behind her. 'What exactly have you against me?' Melanie's quivering tones reflected the anger that consumed her. 'What do you expect to gain by making me appear a thief?'

Undoubtedly Olga was disconcerted at this unexpected visit, and her face had gone a trifle grey. But she endeavoured to bluster her way out of the situation by feigning surprise and saying she had no idea what Melanie meant.

'As we're quite alone your pretence is ridiculous, to say the least,' pointed out Melanie in terse and scornful tones. 'When I was in Lean's office I accused you of lying, and now I'm repeating that accusation. What was your object in telling him you'd found Mrs. Skonson's earrings in my room?'

'Lean. . . .' Olga's dark eyes glinted with something akin to venom. 'Why aren't you sacked? Why didn't he dismiss you instantly? He would have done so had it been anyone else?'

'You're quite put out by finding me here, aren't you?' Melanie's thoughts were conflicting, for although dismissal would undoubtedly have been welcome, she derived extreme satisfaction from the idea of Olga's having failed in her efforts to bring that dismissal about. 'You haven't answered my question. Why have you gone to these lengths to blacken my character in Lean's eyes?'

The older girl's nostrils quivered at Melanie's use of her employer's Christian name for the second time in a matter of minutes.

'What is there between you and Lean?' she demanded, unaware that the question partly revealed her own desires. 'You knew one another before you came here; that's been obvious to me right from the start. You met in England?'

'We were acquainted.' Despite her outward composure Melanie had a trembling sensation in the region of her heart. She had not expected Olga to ask such pertinent questions. As Lean had not disclosed anything of his past relationship with Melanie, she dreaded his reaction should she herself reveal too much. Melanie veered the subject by asking once again why Olga had deliberately schemed to have her branded a thief.

The other girl's eyes flashed as if she would make another attempt to bluster, but suddenly she slumped in her chair and, watching her closely, Melanie was reminded of Sandra's assertion that Olga possessed some peculiar traits. For the movement, which savoured of resignation, was as unexpected as the words which followed it.

'It seemed a good way of getting rid of you – of getting you away from Lean! He's changed towards me from the moment you set foot in this hotel and I knew you weren't strangers.' Black hatred gleamed from the eyes she turned in Melanie's direction. Olga was losing both dignity and control and she held nothing back. Perhaps it was because she owned to herself that prevarication was useless as Melanie had probably guessed at what lay at the root of her schemings. 'There was some mystery, some reason, for his apparent indifference to you – and it *was* only apparent,' she added, but did not for the moment expand on that. 'I didn't want to solve the mystery, I just wanted to see you go – out of Lean's life. I tried to make him sack you, but he merely shrugged when I complained of your sloth and the dirty, untidy method you had of working—' She broke off as Melanie's eyes flashed her indignation, but immediately continued, 'I realized he'd never dismiss you for any minor reason, but knew he would never overlook a theft from one of the guests.' She went on to say the idea had sprung from the conversation she overheard in Mrs. Skonson's bedroom between Melanie and her friend. Melanie gave an audible gasp at the admission, but before she could find anything to say Olga was speaking again. 'What were you and Lean to one another? And why hasn't he told you to go?' She didn't expect an answer, for she went on, 'He's drifting away from me – far away, and before you came he was mine – *mine*, do you hear!'

The woman was in the grip of an intense and all-consuming passion, for little beads of perspiration stood out on her temples and at the sides of her mouth.

'You imagine things,' submitted Melanie, 'when you imply that Lean's not been the same since I came here. My presence can't in any way affect your relationship with him. If, as you say, he's – gone far away, then it's no fault of mine.' She had come here with fury burning inside her, ready and determined to treat Olga with the scorn and condemnation she deserved. But somehow the sight of her, slumped in that chair, her face contorted and her eyes dark with jealousy and hate, but at the same time glazed with a sort of dull despair, served as a brake to Melanie's wrath and she could not bring herself to carry out her original intention. It was quite ridiculous, but she actually felt sorry for the woman. 'It was so unnecessary to go to these lengths, for Lean has no interest in me whatsoever.'

'You're wrong!' Again Olga seemed unable to hold anything back as she went on, 'He watches you – at lunch times from his window – when you're in the garden!' She spoke wildly, her voice reaching a strident pitch that grated on Melanie's ears. 'He watches you if you sunbathe – as you sometimes do on Sundays . . . and he wants you—'

'Nonsense!' Melanie realized her pulse was racing. For one fleeting second she was in her fiancé's arms, yielding to his kisses, thrilled yet terrified by the intensity of a desire manfully suppressed. 'Why should Lean watch me?'

'That's just it – why? He wants you, I know it!'

'Olga!' Involuntarily the girl's name slipped out. 'Are you crazy? Pull yourself together. You don't know what you're saying!'

'I know what my eyes can see!' Her face was white and the beads of perspiration were more pronounced than ever. 'What was there between you before? Why did you part—? No, don't interrupt! He has something against you, it's obvious, but he – he wants y-you . . .' Her voice dropped to a whisper and Melanie thought at first that she experienced a choking feeling resulting from the strength of her emotions, but to her amazement she realized it was a sob that had halted Olga's words. 'Go away! It was me he wanted until you came – me!'

Her face as white as Olga's, Melanie advanced into the middle of the room and stood with her hands resting on the back of the chair, for she felt she needed support. Olga's assertions had shaken her to the very core even though she felt they sprang from her jealous imagination. For only now did the astounding revelation come to her that she had never really forgotten Lean. Only at this moment did she stop to ask herself why there had never been another man in her life since the moment Lean had left her, with ringing in her ears that warning uttered in tones vibrating with bitterness and hate. She had given up the boy who had supplanted Lean, given him up instantly and thrown herself into work and study, determined to break away from the fruitless round and find fulfilment in a career. And what of Richard? For a long while he had merely been her boss, but then he had suddenly noticed her as a woman. Some sort of relationship had developed .... but Melanie now knew it was one-sided. Had he proposed she would have given him a definite no for an answer.

Aware that Olga was more controlled and awaiting some response from her, Melanie said she was allowing her imagination to run away with her, that she, Melanie, was no more to Lean than any other of his employees. And then she added grimly,

'Also, thanks to you, he considers me to be a thief, so I don't think there's the remotest possibility of his switching his affections from you to me.'

Switching his affections. .... What were his feelings for Olga? Sandra had believed her to be no more than a diversion – although she had later qualified that saying he might marry her, Melanie recalled, frowning.

'Yes, yes, I'm sure you're right and I have been imagining things.' Olga spoke in her customary arrogant way; it was plain that she had fully recovered from the violent impact of her emotions, and if she regretted her loss of control she did not appear unduly embarrassed by it. 'If I were in your shoes,' she added baldly, 'I'd leave without waiting to be sacked.'

A faint smile touched the corners of Melanie's mouth.

'But then you're not in my shoes, are you?' she said, and without giving Olga the opportunity to say anything to that quietly left the room.

For a while Melanie debated on whether or not to go back to Lean and tell him of the admission Olga had just made concerning the theft of the earrings, but she abandoned the idea. Olga would deny everything and she, Melanie, would merely be subjected to further embarrassment.

'It isn't all that important,' she told Sandra resignedly. 'So long as it's kept from the rest of the staff I don't care. Lean's opinion of me was as low as it could be before this happened; he told me that a short while ago.' It was the following day and Melanie had come to Sandra's room for the coffee break, having taken her at her word about using her room just whenever she wanted. For it was almost impossible to sit in her own room; not only was it necessary to have on the electric light all the time, but now that the weather had warmed up the air in that tiny space was always stifling. 'Mrs. Skonson's had her earrings returned, you say?'

Sandra nodded a little disgustedly.

'They're lying on her dressing-table again this morning! I expect he returned them to her himself explaining that they'd been stolen and asking her to keep quiet about it. She would, I'll admit that, because she's awfully nice . . . though she looked a trifle suspiciously at me,' went on Sandra reflectively. 'Do you know something, Melanie – it's now struck me that she thinks I'm the guilty party.'

'No – oh, I'm sure you're wrong.' Melanie felt distressed – and strangely guilty. 'I'm terribly sorry if that's the case—'

'Don't worry yourself about it,' cut in Sandra carelessly. 'I'm not in the least troubled about Mrs. Skonson's opinion of me.' She shrugged and went off into the kitchen to make the coffee. 'In any case, she'll be gone in a day or two and I'll never set eyes on her again.'

'But you'll lose such a good tip,' Melanie pointed out, still faintly distressed at the idea of Sandra's being regarded as a thief by the woman who would have tipped her most generously.

'Perhaps.' Sandra merely laughed at Melanie, who had followed her into the kitchen and was reaching for the tray. 'Don't worry, I've said. A tip's lost, so who cares? Some don't tip – think they've done enough when they've paid the ten per cent. Come, let's have our coffee on the balcony. My vine's growing right over the supports now and I've a lovely shady corner.' Sandra had two very comfortable garden chairs which she had 'snaffled' from the terrace down below. She also had a small wicker table which she had actually taken from the lounge. There were dozens, she had said, so one would never be missed.

'I believe in making myself comfortable.' Sandra gave a continued sigh as she sat down under the shade of the vine. 'You're stupid, putting up with that room as it is. I'd at least have a rug on the floor and some decent furniture around me.'

Melanie's mouth curved bitterly.

'And be hauled into Lean's office on another charge of theft?'

'It wouldn't be theft – merely borrowing.' Sandra poured the coffee and placed Melanie's cup on the table beside her. 'Have a biscuit.' From the trees came the continuous chirping of the crickets; day and night it went on, ceaselessly. There was never a moment of complete silence. Suddenly the noise of the insects was lost as a loud and imperious knock sounded on the outer door. 'Who can that be?' frowned Sandra, rising from her chair. She went through the window and a moment later Melanie heard Olga's voice.

'Have you any idea where Melanie is, Sandra? I must give her some instructions before I go out – and I'm already late. I expected her to be in her room, but she isn't.'

'She's here. Come inside if you want to speak to her.'

The next moment Olga was standing by the window, her eyes kindling strangely at the sight of Melanie sitting there, comfortably enjoying the fresh air and the view.

'I want you to prepare the suite on the first floor, the one Mr. Angeli keeps for his relations and friends. And do the work thoroughly, because I shall examine the rooms myself.' She turned to go and Sandra said conversationally,

'I expect Mr. Angeli's mother's coming. She comes often, doesn't she?'

'She is coming, yes, but not for another week. Mr. Angeli's sister, Eleni, is on her way from England and will be arriving some time tomorrow.'

Eleni! Melanie was suddenly frozen to her chair. She had never met Eleni, and somehow the thought of ever meeting her had not once occurred to her. Had Lean expressly asked that she should do the room?

'Who – who will be looking after the suite later – after this young lady's arrival, I mean?' she inquired breathlessly.

'You will.'

'But it's not in my area—'

'It is now. Mr. Angeli's requested me to tell you you'll be the room maid there while his people are staying with him.' She went out and Sandra turned.

'Eleni . . . that's *the* sister?'

'Yes, that's right.' Melanie's face was pale and her voice low and husky. 'This is simply to humiliate me even further.'

'You haven't met this Eleni your brother was engaged to?'

'We didn't even know she existed until Gerard made his confession.' She looked up distractedly. 'He's hate-

74

ful to make me look after her. I'm going to feel dreadful!'

'His action's certainly calculated to cause you embarrassment.' Sandra paused, then murmured thoughtfully, 'Doesn't it strike you as odd that he goes to these lengths to – well, to hurt you?'

'There's nothing odd about it. He hates me and for years he's been nursing the desire for revenge. Eleni's coming just provides him with an added opportunity for getting his own back on me for what I did to him all those years ago.'

Sandra was shaking her head in a sort of mechanical gesture, as if she were still lost in thought.

'It seems so out of character, for he's away up there on a lofty pedestal, aloof and so superior. I'd have thought his attitude would have been one of complete indifference. A man doesn't normally remember a slight for such a long time – not unless. . . .'

'Yes?' Melanie shot her a glance of inquiry. 'Unless what?'

A small sigh was Sandra's only response for a while; plainly she hesitated in voicing her thoughts and when she did eventually speak Melanie gained the impression that she was holding something back.

'I think his hurt must have gone very deep, Melanie, for him to harbour animosity for so long a time. True, he told you on parting that he'd pay you back if ever he had the chance – but that's such a while ago. People usually forget. Frankly, his whole attitude towards you baffles me.'

'The hurt must have gone very deep?' Melanie spoke almost to herself. 'You – you think he l-loved me very much?'

'I think,' replied her friend without any hesitation, 'that you were the world's greatest fool to give him up.'

75

CHAPTER FIVE

ELENI was dark and pretty, with black hair like her brother's and wide soulful eyes. She was highly intelligent too, speaking English with an accent even less pronounced than that of her brother.

Her manner towards Melanie was rather different from what she had expected. True, Eleni was cool and slightly disdainful, but she had none of her brother's arrogance and frigid austerity.

'When you unpack, be very careful,' she warned Melanie. 'I've brought some pieces of cut glass for my brother and they are among my clothes. Do not break them, please.' She was watching Melanie curiously as she spoke, and after thoroughly examining her face she let her eyes wander over Melanie's slim figure before finally coming to rest on her face again. 'I didn't expect you to be like this,' she said, seeming all at once to become rather shy and diffident. 'Lean did not say you were so young . . . or so beautiful.'

Melanie flushed and turned away, picking up the smaller of the cases and putting it on the bed.

'Do you want me to leave anything out for this evening?' she asked quietly. 'You are probably aware that dinner will be served in less than an hour.'

'Yes, I know what time the dinner is served here. You can leave my green cocktail dress on the bed, please, and you'll find shoes and an evening bag to match.' Eleni turned at the door. 'Later when you come to turn down the bed-covers, will you spray the room?' A small laugh broke from her sweet and childish lips. 'I've lived in England, as you know, and always when I come here the insects terrify me. If I have one big moth flying around, or see one of those great beetles, I'll scream!'

Melanie smiled in response to Eleni's laugh, and assured her that the room would be thoroughly sprayed.

Melanie had just finished Eleni's unpacking when Kyrios came to inform her that she must go along to the office. Lean was sitting at his desk, absorbed in some writing, and he kept her there some minutes before saying, as he looked up from his work,

'I believe your morning coffee break is from ten to half past?'

'Yes, that's right.' Melanie glanced at him in some puzzlement.

'From now on it will be from half past ten until eleven o'clock.'

No explanation ... Melanie did not require one.

'Is that all?' Their eyes met – Lean's hard and merciless, Melanie's dull with resignation.

'Not quite. Your lunch break will be later – from one until two.'

'And my tea break?' she questioned tartly. Sandra did not have a tea break, finishing work at four o'clock as she did.

'You may take your tea break at whatever time you wish.'

Melanie hesitated, and then,

'About your sister – the new girl could very well look after her. I have plenty to do without that extra work.'

Lean's eyes flickered perceptively.

'Embarrassing for you, is it? You know why I've put you to serve Eleni—?' He stopped as her eyes flashed, and a half-sneer accentuated the arrogant line of his mouth. 'It hurts, does it, to think of yourself as a servant?'

'You're deriving a great deal of satisfaction from

this, aren't you?' She looked straight at him, unaware that in her own eyes too there lay a hint of contempt. 'Your every move is calculated to inflict further humiliation on me; you gloat on my degradation. But I think, Lean, that someday you might come to despise yourself.' His name slipped out quite naturally; no warning flash of his eyes followed and she wondered if he had heard. For he appeared to be absorbed in reading what he had written ... and yet his hand resting on the desk was slowly opening and closing as if the action were a release for some emotion that had long been caged. She moved quietly to the door, turning as she reached it. Lean never so much as glanced up.

Sandra was furious, but there was nothing either girl could do.

'Well, you must still come in here for your break, and for your lunch if you wish. He can't prevent you from doing that.'

'It's so petty.' Melanie frowned in thought. How he must hate her to act in this way. And as for Olga, it was a pity she had nothing else to do than go running to Lean with every little bit of gossip.

'He certainly has a down on you,' returned Sandra with a shake of her head. 'He means you to be just about as miserable as he can make you.' Sandra was still angry and suddenly she said that Melanie's lot would be made a little easier were she to have a little comfort in her bedroom.

'Its possibilities are limited,' she acknowledged as Melanie began to shake her head. 'But it could be made a little more comfortable. Just you leave it to Auntie Sandra; she'll have a good scrounge around when there's no one about!'

'It doesn't matter. I'll still have my lunch in the garden, and I can have my coffee there, for that matter.'

'That's up to you, but I'm still going to fix that room for you—— It doesn't mean you're to stay up there in the evening. You must still use my place just as much as you like.'

'Thanks, Sandra.' Melanie glanced gratefully at her. 'Don't trouble yourself about the room; I'm never in it except for sleeping. And I'm ever so grateful for the use of your bathroom. That place up there fairly gives me the creeps.'

But, true to her word, Sandra went in search of furniture and rugs for Melanie's room, and one night, on her return from giving Androula her lesson, she glanced around disbelievingly. Two goatskin rugs on the flagstone floor; one rush-seated chair beautifully carved; a more comfortable-looking chair attractively upholstered and a small bookcase-cum-chest of drawers which was to serve as a dressing-table, for on the wall above it was a gilt-framed mirror.

'Where did you get them all?' she inquired of Sandra the following morning as they breakfasted together in the kitchen.

'From various sources,' she shrugged. 'I'm used to helping myself to a few home comforts. In some of these hotels they give you an iron hospital bed and a chest of drawers and that's your lot! Not for Sandra, though, I can always manage to get myself fixed up with something. I'd have got you a smashing dressing-table, but it would never have gone up those narrow winding stairs. If it had, you and I would have taken it up at dead of night.'

Melanie had to laugh, even though she felt a tinge of trepidation at the idea of Olga's deciding to go up to her room and take a look around. After a little while she just had to voice her fears to her friend.

'She won't go up there. Why should she?'

'She went up before.'

'Had to – because of her dastardly little plan to have you appear a thief. There's no reason for her to go up there now, though.'

That was true; there really wasn't any risk. And Melanie never thought for one moment that any risk attached to her hiding the money she made from her English lessons. She had eighteen pounds secreted away in a hole in the wall over which she had placed the photograph of her mother and father which she especially treasured. The hole was half filled with plaster and rubble and some of this was used to cover the small plastic bag in which Melanie kept the precious money that was to help buy her freedom.

'Androula said last night that she and Kostagis wanted to take me out on Sunday,' Melanie told Sandra as, having finished their breakfast, they made their way upstairs together. 'I wondered if you'd like to come? I haven't suggested it to Androula because I didn't know what you'd be doing. But I'm going again tomorrow evening and I can ask if you can come. Androula won't mind at all – in fact, she'll be glad, for there'll be more opportunity for her to hear English spoken, and join in, of course.' They were on the landing and Melanie happened to glance down. Lean was just coming in from his early morning swim and he had a towel knotted round his waist. How bronzed he was! And how slim and athletic-looking. It was said that certain Cretans had inherited that slender, athletic build of their Minoan ancestors. This certainly applied to Lean, Melanie decided, her eyes becoming fixed and pensive as she watched him move towards the door leading to the suite of rooms on the ground floor which he kept for his own use. She was the world's greatest fool to give him up, Sandra had said, and a frown came suddenly to Melanie's brow. Marriage to this man would be far from pleasant. He was too austere and cold, too inaccessible. Again she asked if this change would have come about had she married him. Seven years ago he had been softer, more . . . human. . . .

'I'd love to come.' Sandra's eager voice broke into her reverie and she brought her gaze away from the man to whom she had once been engaged, and who now was her sworn enemy.

'I'll mention it, then?'

'Please. Where are they going – do you know?'

Melanie shook her head.

'Kostagis must decide, of course.'

'Of course!' Sandra gave a wry smile. 'Here, the man always decides. The woman's nothing in the East; she's a useful possession and that's about all.'

'That's only the peasantry, though. There's a change going on – in Greece, at least.'

'With people like Kostagis and Androula, yes. The woman's status is a little higher. But she's still not an equal, not by any means.' Sandra cocked an amused eye at her friend as she added, 'Do you ever think about your life . . . had you married the boss? You'd have been like Androula – sort of half and half; that is, not an equal and yet not completely subdued.'

'Lean always treated me as an equal,' she reflected. 'But of course he was much younger then – and so very different.'

'Nicer – naturally?'

A long pause followed as Melanie dwelt on that.

'Much nicer. He's become dreadfully hard. I find it difficult to believe he's the same man.'

'Perhaps,' returned Sandra after a pause, 'he finds it difficult to believe you are the same woman.'

Melanie's eyes opened wide. The idea had not previously occurred to her.

'I expect he does,' she agreed in tones of vague wonderment. 'And yet he is punishing me as I was then

– I mean,' she added in an attempt at elucidation, 'he's punishing that other girl.'

Sandra's eyes lit with amusement.

'You're saying you've improved with time?'

'I hope I have,' came the fervent reply as Melanie glanced down to the floor below. The door leading to Lean's apartments was just closing behind him.

'You've changed, and he's changed. A different man and a different woman. The man as he is now punishing the woman as she was then. ....' Sandra tailed off musingly and Melanie threw her an interrogating glance. But Sandra merely said on a cryptic note, 'It will be interesting to see what happens when he realizes just what's going on.'

Both Kostagis and his wife were delighted to have Sandra accompany them on the outing the following Sunday.

'We get more practice in our English,' Kostagis said, adding with a laugh, 'And for nothing!'

As they meant to make a whole day of it they took a picnic lunch provided by Kostagis and daintily packed by the little Greek maid who worked for him.

'I think we go for a drive first,' Kostagis suggested, glancing from Melanie to Sandra, but not inviting his wife to contribute to their plans. 'And then perhaps we go to Knossos. Is that all right with you?'

'That'll be marvellous,' returned Sandra enthusiastically. 'Melanie, you've not yet been to Knossos?'

'I walked it once, on my second Sunday, it was. But I didn't start out early enough and had to make my way back before I'd even looked at the palace, because it was getting dark so quickly.'

'You need a long time to look at Palace of Knossos,' put in Androula. 'We go many visits and still haven't seen much? – all?' She smilingly looked to Melanie for the correct word. Melanie obliged but added,

'You say "pay" many visits, Androula.'

The Greek girl frowned.

'Pay? But I pay bill – or pay for food, in shop.'

'Strikes me you earn your money on this English lark,' submitted Sandra, in an undertone. 'How do you propose to explain that one?'

Melanie did not try.

'Let us just say you visited the palace many times. It sounds much better.'

'You very good teacher,' said Kostagis, and already there was a note of loyalty in his voice. Melanie could quite imagine his declaring to his friends that his 'teacher' was better than theirs.

They were out before eight o'clock, driving in brilliant sunshine; a breeze blew in through the open windows of the car, making the journey much more pleasant than it might otherwise have been.

'I'm just wondering,' said Sandra immediately they were on their way, 'if it would be better to visit the palace first. We'd have it to ourselves at this time of the morning.' She and Melanie occupied the back seat of the car and Kostagis turned his head right round. Melanie held her breath. The Greeks often ran such risks, but this being the first time Melanie had experienced it she found herself willing Kostagis to return his attention to the road.

'You like palace to yourselves?' he queried in amazement. The Greeks were a gregarious race and Kostagis could not understand this desire for an avoidance of the tourist crowds.

'We'd enjoy it better, Kostagis,' Melanie told him, but added that he must choose.

'We go now – if you enjoy it more, because this is the day for your pleasure.'

Both girls thanked him and ten minutes later, the car

parked, they were strolling through the gate, past the bust of Sir Arthur Evans, that renowned archaeologist who had thrown himself wholeheartedly into the stupendous task of uncovering the vast and magnificent Palace of King Minos, the supreme ruler of Knossos. Through the accumulated loess and rock waste of centuries Sir Arthur and his many assistants had tirelessly worked their way, uncovering bit by bit treasures like the steatite bull's head and the faience plaques, the ivory acrobat and the famous Town Mosaic, all of which were now in the museum. Room after room was uncovered and it was seen that luxuriously appointed bathrooms had effective plumbing, that the apartments were tastefully and lavishly furnished, that there were shady courtyards, vast store rooms and a Grand Staircase.

'Some people say that Sir Arthur did not do reconstructions well,' Kostagis told them as they stood before the impressive propylaea beyond which was the massive Central Court. Behind the foremost hills rose the heights of Jouctas, sacred mountain of the Minoans, embodying the great goddess Mother Earth. At that time much pagan ritual would be conducted in her honour, and so the palace had been built to enhance the aspect of the holy mountain. 'But we in Crete are grateful to Sir Arthur for all his work and the money he spent.'

'Well they might be,' was Sandra's whispered comment to her friend. 'This place is obviously a great source of wealth to the island. They must get thousands of tourists every year.'

'Aren't we lucky!' exclaimed Melanie some time later as they all stood in the throne room. 'Just imagine – I can sit on that throne, where King Minos sat, three thousand years ago!' She suited action to her words and out came Sandra's camera.

'No use,' Sandra shook her head as she brought Melanie into focus. 'You're covering it all. This Minos,' she said turning to Kostagis. 'He must have been very small?'

'Five feet only were the Minoans, but very athletic figures they had, and the – what you say? – narrow waists, like bee.'

'Wasp-waists – yes, so I've noticed, by the frescoes on the walls.'

They wandered from one great apartment to another, and with Kostagis as their guide it was possible to get the feel of the past grandeur and intricacies of the great palace, this house of the Double Axe.

'It's quite incredible, but the plumbing and drainage system appears to have been as effective as any we have today,' Melanie remarked as they stood in the Queen's apartment. 'They seem to have been very concerned with hygiene.'

'Hygiene?' Androula picked that up immediately and Melanie carefully explained.

'Yes, very clean people,' Kostagis put in. 'Not like later. The Greeks later not so clean and – and hygienic.'

'And they were so clever at planning,' Melanie continued as they moved about. 'The central courtyard here is the heart of the palace, I take it?' She glanced at Kostagis and he nodded.

'This plan typifies the Minoan palace,' he went on to explain. 'Always they have a central courtyard; this was used for ceremonies conducted by the king, for religious – er – what you say?'

'Rites – rituals?'

'That is it – rituals.' He shrugged as he glanced around. 'And I think they would have moonlight strolls with the lady-friend also.'

'There are ever so many altars,' Sandra remarked.

'Were they always offering sacrifices?'

'Many times they offer the sacrifice. This sort of palace was not only the home of the king, but also it was the centre of the Sacred Precincts, so you have many altars and shrines. And chapels too, and soon we will see the baths for ritual – er – cleaning?'

'Purification is the word you want, I think,' offered Sandra, grinning at her friend. 'How much commission do I get?'

'These people – they like much the dance.' Androula pointed to one of the frescoes on the wall. 'They look to me as if they like to dance. I think they had much of the joy.'

Certainly a volatile race, thought Melanie, examining the fresco indicated by Androula.

'Yes, they were a carefree, happy people,' she agreed. 'And very fond, I should imagine, of demonstrating their athletic prowess.'

'Bull-baiting – they very much like this sport.' The beautiful bull-baiting frescoes were the most famous, and all these depicted the graceful bodily strength of the Minoans. They had a certain facial beauty too, with delicate bone structure and attractive almond-shaped eyes.

'Just imagine the girls taking part in that dangerous sport. What exactly went on, Kostagis?'

They were sitting on the remains of a wall, high on an upper floor and a breathtaking panorama spread in an arc before them. It was a landscape formed of concave and convex slopes with here and there a deep ravine and the outlines of Jouctas engraved on the pure blue Grecian sky.

Bull-baiting was a skilled and highly dangerous sport, Kostagis began to explain, and both sexes loved to exhibit their prowess. From the frescoes, many of which were in the museum, it was easy to form an accurate picture of what had occurred. The youth or maiden would wait for the charging bull, grasp its lowered horns and as the bull charged he or she would be tossed into the air. The clever part was to know the exact second when to release the hold on the beast's horns, turn a somersault and land on the animal's back. Then before it could charge again the boy or girl must leap nimbly from the bull's back and land safely on the ground.

'So they didn't kill the bull, or even hurt it,' Melanie said with a sigh of relief that brought a smile to the faces of the other three.

Kostagis shrugged apologetically.

'They later sacrificed the bull.'

'Sad ending,' laughed Sandra. 'Kostagis is sorry for your disappointment. We don't need any language to tell us that.'

The two girls laughed, but the Greek couple just looked on, puzzled. Melanie decided to explain and Kostagis considered it a huge joke that his feelings were so plainly revealed by his expression.

'I think it's a good suggestion that we now go to one of those cafés we passed and have some refreshments,' said Kostagis a little while later. They were still wandering about the upper floors; the sun was climbing and the air was stifling despite the breeze coming down from the mountains. The aspect of so much variation of colour took Melanie's breath away. Corn poppies of brilliant scarlet, the gold of crown daisies and the blue of borage. The silver-grey of olives against the mountainside, the darker silhouette of the cypresses . . . the tantalizing, indescribable green of the polished vine leaves.

They all agreed about the refreshments and left the vast palace with Melanie having the impression that one could come each day for a month and not see everything. There were so many courts and apartments, numerous shady walks and lightwells, colonnades and stairways, storerooms where the massive earthenware jars instantly brought to mind the story of Ali Baba and the Forty Thieves.

'It's not difficult to see how the myth of the Labyrinth originated,' said Melanie as they sat on a vine-shaded terrace outside the café, drinking Turkish coffee from minute cups. 'The palace is so vast and sprawling, with its array of rooms and courts, one on top of another, and the corridors and endless apartments, that it would appear labyrinthine to the gullible peasants and serfs of Crete, and so we get the myth of the Labyrinth and the monstrous Minotaur.'

'He was born because of the desire of the queen to have a child by the sacred white bull consecrated to the moon,' Kostagis informed them. 'Minos her husband was very angry when the bull-headed son arrived—'

'You can't exactly blame him for that,' interrupted Sandra with a laugh. 'So he flung him in the cellars, so I've heard?'

'King Minos have the Labyrinth made specially. The Minotaur live in there and every nine years seven beautiful maidens and seven youths from Athens were thrown in for him to devour.'

'Then Theseus slew the monster and was led out of the Labyrinth by the lovely Ariadne.'

'And so we do have a happy ending this time,' said Sandra, glancing with some amusement at her friend.

But Melanie was shaking her head. 'Theseus left the lovely daughter of King Minos behind on the barren island of Dia after having spent the night with her there.'

'Very bad it was,' laughed Androula. 'Theseus bad man.'

'Very bad man,' agreed Sandra. 'But men are like that.'

To the girls' surprise Kostagis's eyes suddenly blazed.

'Men not like that! And in any case, Theseus was not from Crete. In Crete man never leave his wife – or even his betrothed!'

'Never?' Sandra looked sceptically at him. 'You have broken engagements like anybody else.'

'No! When Cretan love he love for ever.' Vigorously Kostagis shook his head, while Androula merely nodded at the girls, but in agreement with her husband all the same. 'Cretan man love once, and this woman he stays with always!'

'Cretan man love once. . . .' Sandra cast Melanie a strange glance from under her lashes. 'When a Cretan loves he loves for ever?'

'That's what I said.' Kostagis put up a finger and wagged it in Sandra's face. 'When I met Androula I knew – that minute – that she was for my wife.'

'The moment you set eyes on her?' Melanie's voice was unsteady and she regarded Kostagis with something akin to awe. 'Not as quickly as that?'

'It is not so strange,' he answered with a shrug. 'People are – what you say? – drawn. And with a Cretan this is very strong. He knows his own mind – and he never changes it.'

Without moving her head Melanie sent a flickering glance in Sandra's direction. Sandra's face was expressionless and Melanie looked away again, wondering at the sudden turbulence within her.

They took their picnic lunch by the roadside, under the shade of the carob trees, and as it was still quite early when they had finished Androula suggested they take the girls to see another palace, that at Mallia.

'You would like that?' Kostagis glanced from one

girl to the other. 'It's a nice drive and we've plenty of time.'

The girls agreed, and a most pleasant and interesting drive it was. The fascinating colour spread of the landscape with its greens and silver-greys above a carpet of scarlet and gold; the iridescent aquamarine of the sea quivering under the serenity of an azure sky – all this was a memorable part of the journey, as was the band of gypsies they passed, untouched by time as they travelled on their mule carts, carrying all their worldly possessions with them. On one side of the Plain of Mallia rose the Lasithi Mountains, while on the Plain of itself were scattered orange and olive groves, banana plantations and vineyards.

They reached Mallia and, with the Greek's inevitable thirst for Turkish coffee, Kostagis stopped at a little roadside café and ordered refreshments.

The girls were fascinated by the village, exclaiming all the time as they wandered through the twisting little streets, meeting now and then a woman on a donkey, but no vehicles for the paths were far too narrow.

'How marvellous not to have traffic.' Sandra stopped in the middle of the road and stood viewing with admiration the little whitewashed cottage with its flower-laden courtyard shaded with vines and tumbling masses of purple bougainvillea.

'No cars can come in these narrow lanes.' Kostagis and Androula stopped beside Sandra, but Melanie's attention was arrested by a woman on a donkey, riding side-saddle and crossing herself as she passed a niche in the village street. She smiled at Melanie and moved on, her face brown and lined, yet possessed of a dignity and grace seen only in the women of Crete. The way she held herself on the donkey's back, her upright posture and the complete serenity of her whole bearing seemed to reflect the dignity and pride of her Minoan ancestors.

Lean intruded into Melanie's thoughts, bringing a return of that disturbance within her. She could not analyse her feelings . . . and for some incomprehensible reason she did not want to analyse them. For during the past few days a restlessness had begun slowly to possess her – impalpable at first like some vague and abstract thing tugging at her subconscious, but gradually taking form so that it was now not only tangible but also troublesome.

'Welcome to our village.' Startled, Melanie turned. An old man wearing the black and dusty *vraga* was smiling and holding out his hand. She took it, felt the roughness of the skin and deformation of the bones. A hand that toiled, that scraped at the dry brown earth to provide its owner with a subsistence living. Where had such a man learned English? she wondered, her surprise increasing as he went on to invite them to his house. 'My wife and children will be very pleased to see you.'

The house was really no more than a hovel, but what was lacking in refinements was more than compensated for in the hospitality of its owners.

Maria and Kosta, the lovely brown children of Niko and Helena Stephanides, came eagerly from the court-yard to smile at the strangers – or guests as they all were, for in Greek the word 'stranger' means also 'guest'. And so every stranger in Greece is treated as a guest, and an honoured one at that. Lavished on the four were drinks and sweetmeats, fruit and cakes and even souvenirs.

The interior of the one-storeyed stone house was cool and dark, the only light coming from the open door-way, for all the shutters were closed against the excessive heat and glare of the sun. The floor was flagged and, noticing that the children ran about barefoot, Melanie stooped and touched the stones.

'There might be under-floor heating!' she exclaimed. 'Just feel these flagstones, Sandra.'

'It is always so at this time of the year,' Androula smiled, her lovely brown eyes twinkling with amusement at the surprise on Melanie's face. 'We not have carpets and rugs as in England.'

'You are going to see the Palace of Mallia?' Nico asked, drinking .with apparent relish the deadly *raki*, which was even more distasteful to Melanie than the aniseed-flavoured *ouzo*.

'We're intending to have a look, yes.' Kostagis glanced at Helena and said something in Greek to Nico, who shook his head.

'Helena does not speak much English – just greetings and thanks. I learnt at school, and also I was in England for six years, working.'

Melanie was on the wooden bench, with Kosta on one side of her and Maria on the other. They had out the family album and every time Maria saw her father's photograph she would point to it and say, 'Papa'. Obviously she was very proud of him, for she kept on like this until every picture in the album had been shown to Melanie.

There were waves and smiles as they all departed, the three girls each with a posy of flowers and Kostagis carrying a rose between his teeth.

For over an hour they wandered round the palace, which was Minoan like Knossos but not nearly so extensive in area. Here the sacred mountain was Dikte, in which was the cave where Rhea gave birth to the mighty Zeus.

It was eight o'clock when they returned to the Hotel Avra. Eleni was just getting into a taxi and a few seconds later it purred away from the hotel entrance.

'I didn't know *he* was with us!' The sharpness of Sandra's voice brought Melanie's head round with a jerk. 'How long has Alec Helsby been staying here?'

'Since yesterday.' For some reason Melanie found herself trembling slightly. 'He seems charming, but obviously you've met him before?'

'At a hotel in Rome where I once worked. He was staying there and he took a young girl out one evening – without her parents' knowledge – and, well–' She broke off and Melanie's trembling increased. 'There was a big scandal, because the parents fetched in the police. He's a rogue of the most detestable kind. It came out that he just goes around preying on these innocent young girls – and he finds it easy, I suppose, because as you say, on the surface he's charming.'

'Sandra . . . you think Eleni might not be safe?'

'No girl's safe with him,' Sandra shrugged, and went on to say that although she was perturbed at the idea of Eleni's going out with Alec Helsby, it was none of their business. 'Come on, I'll make some coffee and we'll have a snack supper.'

Melanie frowned at her.

'I'm going to find Lean,' she declared emphatically. 'I don't know what he can do, but it's my duty to repeat to him what you've just said.'

'As you like.' Sandra paused in thought. 'Of course, Eleni might not react in the same way as that other girl. She might not give him any trouble, in which case—'

'Sandra! What are you suggesting? You know as well as I do that Greek girls aren't like that at all.' She twisted her hands distractedly. 'Don't you see how awful it would be for her? – and for her family? She'd never be able to marry!'

'I do know all this,' Sandra answered quietly, 'and you can see the boss if you feel like doing so. But on my travels I've learned to mind my own business. The little hotel servant doesn't go poking her nose into the affairs of her superiors. However, it's a little different with you, having known the boss before. You go and see him and I'll be making the supper.'

CHAPTER SIX

'MR. ANGELI, he go with Miss Newson on visit to friends,' Kyrios told Melanie when, after searching about for Lean, she inquired of Kyrios if he had any idea where he was. 'They are invited to this house because the friends of his have son home from America. I hear Mr Angeli on phone—'

'Where is this house?' she asked urgently. 'Do you know?'

Kyrios shook his head. He had no idea where the house was, and added,

'He sometimes go to the south of the island to friends, but sometimes he go another place.'

Not very helpful. Melanie stood there, feeling defeated, and yet unwilling just to do nothing.

'I think I'll phone the police,' she told Sandra a few minutes later, but instantly shook her head. 'What can they do?'

'That's just it; what can anyone do? We haven't any idea where they've gone.'

'They were going to dine somewhere,' said Melanie on a sudden note of hope. 'Eleni was wearing a cocktail dress—'

'There are only about forty places they could go to in and within a short distance of Heraklion,' returned Sandra, shaking her head discouragingly. 'Forget it; there's nothing we can do.'

But Melanie could not rest and she said she was going to get a taxi and visit all the better class hotels round about.

'Many of the places can be eliminated, because he'd never take Eleni to a third-rate hotel to dine.' Should she ask Sandra to accompany her? Naturally she would prefer to have her friend, but she hesitated, convinced that Lean would be far from pleased at the idea of them both running round looking for Eleni. As Sandra had said, it was different for Melanie, having known Lean before.

Taking five pounds from her precious savings, Melanie went down and waited for the taxi. Sandra had phoned for it and within minutes it arrived. The driver looked at Melanie a trifle suspiciously when she stated her request, but he soon threw himself into what he obviously considered to be a game – and a very profitable game, for the search promised to continue for hours.

'No luck?' he asked for about the twentieth time, as Melanie emerged from the hotel. She shook her head. They had left the main part of the town and were now circling round outside it.

'Where are there some really nice hotels, not too far from Heraklion?' She heaved a sigh as the question left her lips, for there was no knowing in which direction Eleni and her escort might have gone. 'Where is an – an – intimate sort of hotel?'

'Intimate?' The driver frowned at her as he reached for the inevitable cigarette and, putting it in his mouth, searched in another pocket for a lighter. 'What is this – intimate?'

With a sinking feeling in the pit of her stomach she got back into the taxi and told the driver to stop at every hotel to which he came. It was ten o'clock and her heart was racing all the time as she allowed her imagination to run riot. If only Lean had been in he would, she felt sure, have known what to do. But then he had influence and the police would have hastened to do his bidding. Police would have been at every hotel within minutes of his ringing up the police station.

'This one nice – eating outside by the sea.' The driver pulled up and once again Melanie made her inquiries at the hotel desk.

'A Greek girl with an Englishman? She have on white dress?'

'Yes,' Melanie returned breathlessly. 'She's here?'

'No, madam.' The manager beckoned a passing waiter and spoke to him in Greek. 'Yes, they were having dinner. But they go now and the waiter he say they have taxi. He say they go one half-hour back.'

Melanie's heart sank again.

'You don't know where they went? No, of course you wouldn't.'

Aware of her distress, the manager spoke again to the waiter.

'The Englishman, he was persuading the girl to go and see some friends of his— Excuse me a moment, please.' He questioned the waiter once more, nodding and saying *nai* over and over again, bringing a gleam of hope to Melanie's eyes. 'Yes, well, this waiter say the man tells the girl his friends are English and have come from London to live in Crete. He tell the girl that they will like very much to meet her. The waiter says the girl said yes, but she must be back with her—' Again he begged her pardon and talked with the waiter. 'She have to be back with her brother at half past ten.' He glanced at his watch. 'So, madam, I expect the girl will now be with her brother.'

But Melanie shook her head. If Alec Helsby had friends in Crete then obviously he would be staying with them.

'They took a taxi, you say—?' Melanie broke off and stared unbelievingly as Giles came into the hotel accompanied by another Englishman.

'Melanie, what are you doing—? He suddenly noticed her pallor and a look of concern entered his eyes.

97

'Is something wrong?'

'Yes, Giles,' she faltered, aware of the odd stares of the hotel manager and the waiter. 'Something's very wrong.' She looked round with a sort of helpless desperation. 'I can't talk here.'

'We've just come in for a drink. This is a friend of mine, Les. Les, meet Melanie.' They shook hands and Giles nodded in the direction of the bar. 'Come, let's hear what it's all about.' He led the way and they followed him to the bar.

'It's a very private matter,' she said, almost in tears. 'I don't know whatever to do!'

'Look here—' Les had sat down on one of the stools, but he got to his feet again. 'I'm going. I'll see you tomorrow, Giles. Good night, Melanie.'

'Oh, but—'

'Thanks, Les. It's all right, Melanie, Les doesn't mind. Very understanding chap. Now, out with it.'

She told him what had happened, half afraid of Lean's anger when he knew of this confidence, and yet unable to resist the temptation of talking to someone.

'The damned scoundrel!' he exclaimed when she had finished. 'They've been gone half an hour, you say?'

'Over half an hour, Giles. And – and I know I'm never going to find her now!'

'Hold on, Melanie. No need for you to get so upset. Whatever happens it's not your fault.'

'She's so sweet, you've no idea. I've only known her a few days, but I like her, Giles. She's so – innocent.' She shook her head distractedly. 'What can I do?'

'Let's think about this – no, I have an idea!' He beckoned to the waiter and spoke to him in English. The waiter merely shrugged and Giles began speaking in Greek. 'He knows the taxi-driver. Come, if he's dropped this couple already we might find him.'

'Find him? Where?'

'He frequents the *taverna* just down the road, this fellow says. If he hasn't another fare then that's where he'll be.'

To Melanie's profound relief the taxi driver was sitting there, his cab drawn right up to the table where he and three other men were playing cards. Melanie began to speak, but he did not understand much English and Giles took over. Within seconds they were in the car and speeding along the main road.

'Funny thing, but I know the house,' Giles told her grimly. 'It's been empty for a couple of months and the owner's been trying to let it. This fellow must have rented it from him— The things these rogues get up to!'

'Is it far away?'

'It can't be any more than a couple of miles along here. Then we have to turn off, and it's on a rather lonely lane. It's on its own, too, and I think that's why the chap's had it empty. Tourists don't like to be off the beaten track like that.' He paused and nodded as the driver turned off the main road. 'Yes, it's the one. But how would he convince this girl his friends were there if the place was in total darkness?' He spoke to the taxi-driver and Giles's voice was grimmer than ever as he told Melanie that all the lights were on in the house when the driver took the couple there over half an hour before. 'He must have been there earlier and put them on! He's a clever rogue, this Alec Helsby.'

By the time the car stopped Melanie felt ready to collapse. Her legs were so weak they could scarcely support her as she got out of the car.

'Giles . . . I'm so terrified.'

'Steady on.' Instinctively he took her arm. 'As I've just said, you're not to blame for anything.' The taxi driver was looking at the house, and, as if sensing his expectancy, Giles told him to take the car farther along the road and he would give him a call when he was wanted. 'Far too curious, these Greeks,' he said to Melanie. 'There's nothing offensive, but they're so afraid of missing something.'

The shutters were all closed, but light escaped through those on the side of the house. Without wasting a moment Giles hammered on the front door. Immediately there was a cry and Melanie's heart seemed to leap right into her throat. Were they too late?

'I'm here, Eleni—'

'Melanie!' A small silence and then, 'It's my friend from the hotel, so you'd better let me out!'

My friend. . . .

'Be quiet!'

'Open up,' commanded Giles in a loud and threatening voice. 'Open this door or it'll be broken down!' Turning to Melanie, Giles said that if Alec refused they would have to enlist the aid of the taxi driver.

'Yes – anything. We must get it open!' Melanie had reached the state of panic where she didn't care how many people knew so long as Eleni was brought safely out of this house.

'Get away from here and mind your own business!'

'This is our business. Give the driver a shout, Melanie, and we'll get our shoulders to this door.'

But Alec did not wait for the door to be broken down; the next moment it was thrown wide open and Eleni, whose voice had seemed so steady and composed, flung herself into Melanie's arms and sobbed hysterically.

'How d-did you g-get here? I didn't th-think anyone would – would find me—'

'Hush, darling. We are here and you've nothing to worry about. Come, the taxi's just up the road.'

True to type, Alec revealed only cowardice when threatened with the police, and although his lips were drawn back in an ugly snarl his face was grey and his hands clenched and unclenched in a nervous, spasmodic movement.

'If you return to the Hotel Avra the police will be waiting for you,' Giles lied. But Melanie knew the threat would prove effective and they would never set eyes on Alec Helsby again.

'We could have shouted for the taxi man,' said Giles as he came up to them a moment or two later on the lane. 'But the walk will probably do her good.'

Having partly recovered from her terrifying experience, Eleni thanked her rescuers fervently and then wanted to know how the rescue had come about. She and Melanie were in the back of the taxi and Melanie kept her voice low even though the driver did not understand much English. Eleni regarded the fact of Sandra's having previously known Alec Helsby as something of a miracle. Melanie then asked Eleni what had induced her to go with the man, adding curiously,

'Did Lean know you were dining out with him?'

'Lean expected that I would remain in the hotel like a good little Greek girl, and he's going to be very angry with me. But he forgets I've lived in England and that your ways are now more familiar to me than ours. In England I go out with a gentleman sometimes. . . .' She tailed off and Melanie knew she was thinking of Gerard. Impulsively she said,

'I'm so sorry for everything, Eleni – I can call you Eleni, can't I?'

'I want you to.' Eleni shook her head. 'I was very foolish over Gerard, and he did a bad thing to me, but you are not to blame – I am very sure of that now.'

'What's happened tonight doesn't prove that I'm

honest, Eleni,' she returned with a bitter little smile.

'Since knowing you, which is only a few days, I think there is much that has not been explained. I think Lean is very harsh with you, and I'm hurt inside when you have to work so hard and have no money.'

The two men in front had been conversing in Greek; there was a lull and Melanie waited until they should begin speaking again.

'Lean has obviously told you everything. You know of our broken engagement.' It was a statement and Melanie regretted her words on the instant, for Eleni jerked round in surprise and gave an astonished little gasp.

'You were engaged to my brother! But why – why did you not marry him?'

What a fool she was! Melanie felt so angry with herself that she could not speak for a moment.

'I shouldn't have mentioned it. I took it for granted you knew – that Lean had told you of the way – I—' Melanie bit her lip, having the greatest difficulty with her words. 'I really have no excuse, Eleni; I became engaged to Lean and then threw him over.'

'You—!' It was Eleni's turn to search for words. 'But didn't you love him?'

The question Melanie had now begun to ask herself.

'Frankly, I don't know.' The bald admission brought another gasp to the Greek girl's lips. But she sat in thoughtful silence for a while before saying, her tones strangely edged with regret,

'You might have been my sister-in-law. . . .' She tailed off musingly and then added, 'Lean must have loved you very much to offer marriage, and it's because he was hurt that he now wants to hurt you in return. It's all explained – all that was puzzling me, for I could not understand why Lean was making you pay for your brother's crime.'

'It's only now that I realize just how deeply he was hurt,' Melanie said with difficulty. 'I was seventeen, Eleni, and thoughtless. But that's no excuse, and every day I'm coming to blame Lean less and less for what he's doing to me.'

'I would have liked you for my sister,' said Eleni, and her voice held such sincerity and regret that a lump rose in Melanie's throat. 'We'll always be friends, though, won't we? We're not ever going to lose touch?'

'No, Eleni, we'll never lose touch.'

To Melanie's dismay Lean and Olga were sitting on the verandah when they reached the hotel. The driver had to be paid, and Melanie hesitated. There was no reason why she should not have money of her own – Lean would probably take it for granted that she had brought out sufficient for her needs, yet something warned her not to go up to her room and produce the money for the taxi fare.

'Will you pay the man?' she whispered to Eleni.

'Yes, of course—Oh, I've left my bag in that horrid man's house!' Having risen from his chair, Lean was approaching them, with what could only be described as a scowl darkening his face at the idea of his sister's having been out with Melanie.

'What is this?' he demanded, without even a glance at the taxi driver standing there eager to learn something about this odd situation in which he had taken part.

'Lean,' began Eleni hastily, 'will you pay the driver?'

He produced the money, clearly puzzled as his glance flickered from one girl to the other.

'Where have you been?' he asked as the taxi swung round and disappeared into the road. He suddenly noticed the tear-stains on Eleni's face and added sharply, 'You've been crying.'

Eleni began to speak, saying impulsively that Melanie had rescued her, but Melanie decided to interrupt.

'I should speak to your brother in private,' she recommended quietly, her eyes straying to Olga, who was sitting upright in her chair in an attitude of expectancy and interest. At Melanie's interruption she leant back, resigned, but her resentment was clearly revealed in the dark glance she threw in Melanie's direction.

'Yes, Melanie, of course.' Eleni looked up into the stern and questioning eyes of her brother. 'Shall we go into the sitting-room, Lean?'

By that Eleni meant the room in Lean's private suite, and after bidding Eleni good night Melanie made for the stairs.

'Excuse us, Olga.' Lean smiled at her and then spoke to Melanie. 'You had better come along too. I may be mistaken, but there appears to be some mystery.'

Melanie turned back, following reluctantly as they entered the apartment she had never before seen. Tastefully furnished in the Eastern style, it also contained several paintings and china groups that could be found in any English drawing-room. What caught Melanie's eyes and made her gasp was an exquisite piece of Roman glass – a tear bottle, unmarked by any form of crust which was normally to be found on items unearthed after such eons of time, but filmed with the breathtaking rainbow patina which only age can bring. Unconscious of her act, she moved towards the low shelf on which it stood and before she quite realized it she had put out a finger and touched it, tracing its slender line and texture, revelling in its colouring and marvelling that anything so fragile could survive for two thousand years or more. Perfect. . . . She had seen damaged pieces similar to this, but never one unmarked by even the minutest sign of a crack or a chip.

'I'm sorry.' Her colour fluctuated as she looked up to see the other two watching her with interest. 'It's very beautiful,' she remarked, in a half-hearted endeavour to explain her conduct. 'I have a friend who collects Roman glass.' It was an expensive hobby, but one in which Richard had indulged from the moment of setting eyes on a piece in the museum. How he would love this exquisite little tear bottle, she thought, at the same time vaguely wondering if he would keep his word and come to Crete for his summer holiday.

'Sit down, Melanie.' Lean indicated a chair and she took possession of it. Eleni sat down opposite her, but Lean remained standing, in an attitude of inquiry, as he waited for his sister to begin her explanation. This Eleni did, with a few fearful glances at Lean from under her sweeping dark lashes, yet with more composure than Melanie would have expected. Lean's eyes gradually kindled as Eleni proceeded with her story. Occasionally he flicked an odd glance in Melanie's direction, but instantly his attention would return to his sister as he listened intently to every word that fell from her lips.

Where was the fury? Watching him closely, Melanie marvelled at his calm acceptance of his sister's narrative. Eleni ended by echoing Melanie's own thoughts.

'Aren't you very angry with me, Lean?'

A muscle moved in his throat – the first sign of emotion.

'I'm too relieved at your escape, Eleni.' His voice possessed the vibrant quality of profound thankfulness and Melanie thought of how the Greek girls were protected both by their fathers and their brothers, not normally being allowed out after dark, and never being seen in the *tavernas*, either with or without a male escort.

'I have you to thank,' he said, turning to Melanie. 'And this I do, most sincerely. I hope you'll convey my thanks to your friend – this Giles of whom my sister speaks. Eleni and I are greatly indebted to you both for your prompt action.'

'It was nothing.' Melanie flushed and looked away, embarrassed at being here in this splendid apartment and, strangely, more embarrassed at the idea of Lean's having to show her gratitude. In view of the nature of their relationship it seemed all wrong that he should be compelled to do so. 'May I go now?'

'Not yet.' Eleni looked up coaxingly at her brother. 'I'd like a drink, and I'm sure Melanie could do with one as well. She's been riding round and round for hours.'

'It's all right, Eleni, I don't want a drink.' She rose from her seat, but Lean told her to sit down again. He poured drinks and handed a glass to each of the girls. Then, after pouring himself some wine, he sat down beside his sister.

'This riding round,' he began, with a glance at Melanie. 'I expect you told the taxi driver to come to me for the money?'

'No, I've paid it—' She broke off, dismayed. After her care just now over the second taxi she had blundered over the first.

'Paid it? How much was it?'

'Not very much.' Was it imagination, or was there a hint of suspicion in his eyes?

'Eleni says she left the hotel at eight o'clock. It was half past ten when you found her. How long were you riding round in the first taxi?'

'About two hours,' she admitted.

'Then your fare must have been in the region of four pounds,' he estimated. 'Five if he thought you were a tourist.' Lean waited questioningly for her to give him some explanation about the money, but she remained silent. 'I believe you brought some travellers' cheques with you, but Miss Newson said you'd put them in the safe here?'

'Yes – but I have some other money.' The money in travellers' cheques had been for her necessities; she had thought to spend it bit by bit as required, but on discovering what Lean intended paying her Melanie had determinedly put the money away towards the final settlement. Her resolve not to touch it had been strengthened when, after writing to her brother, she had received the reply that, as he was at present unemployed, he could not contribute towards the debt. At some future date he would repay her, he wrote, but Melanie set no store by that promise. Lean still seemed puzzled, and Melanie recalled the incident of the earrings and felt sure he was wondering if she had come by the money dishonestly. However, there was nothing to be learned from the cool impassivity of his tones when at last he spoke.

'How much was the taxi?'

'It doesn't matter—'

'Of course it does,' interrupted Eleni. 'You're not going to be out of pocket. I expect, as Lean says, he charged you about five pounds.'

'Was it five pounds?' Lean inquired softly when Melanie did not respond.

Reluctantly she admitted she had paid the taxi driver five pounds. She felt guilty – and probably appeared so, she concluded with an unhappy sigh. However, there was still nothing to be gleaned from Lean's voice as he promised to make good the money. Then he asked her to have another drink.

'I don't want anything more, thank you.' Putting down her empty glass, Melanie rose to her feet. 'I'm tired . . . if you'll excuse me . . . ?'

'Good night, Melanie.' Lean looked gravely at her, all hatred for the present dissolved. 'And thank you once again.' She turned away, possessed of some vague yearning that brought with it a regret which she resolutely thrust aside, unwilling to acknowledge its existence even to herself. 'But for your help—' He broke off, reluctant to continue, and turned a stern glance upon his sister. 'You'll accept no more invitations, Eleni. If you want to go out then just say so and I myself shall accompany you.'

'Yes.' It was the first sign of meekness Eleni had shown and it struck Melanie how westernized the whole family was. In the ordinary way Lean would have told Eleni she must stay in and had she objected the request would have been strengthened to an order. On the other hand, Eleni herself would never have dreamed of dining out with a stranger; she would of her own accord have remained within the safety of the hotel.

When Lean sent for Melanie the following morning it was not only to give her the five pounds, but also to tell her she could in future have Wednesday off.

'Will my money be reduced?' The question was out before she could check it and a faint smile touched Lean's mouth.

'No, Melanie, your money will remain the same.'

'I don't need to be rewarded for what I did,' she said with a hint of protest.

'It's my wish that you have Wednesday off,' was Lean's cool comment before, changing the subject, he told her his mother would be arriving the following day and would be sharing Eleni's suite.

The idea of meeting the mother of her ex-fiancé so disturbed Melanie that she felt she must have an answer to a question which had been troubling her from the moment she had known of Madam Angeli's coming visit.

'Does – does your mother know about – about our engagement?'

He stiffened, but his tone was expressionless as he replied,

'My mother knew at the time that I had become engaged to an English girl, and of course I told her your name. She might not have guessed it was you, but you've told Eleni about our engagement. Obviously she'll talk about it to my mother.'

'It was an accident,' she murmured apologetically. 'I was under the impression Eleni already knew.'

To her surprise he merely shrugged his shoulders.

'It doesn't matter. I expect it would have come out eventually.' His eyes flickered as something occurred to him. 'You feel it's going to be embarrassing for you? – having to meet my mother?'

What a strange position in which to be, she thought. Here they were, discussing their broken engagement in the most matter-of-fact way when, at the time, they had both been so emotionally involved – Lean consumed with fury and hate, and Melanie herself reduced to terror by the intensity of a passion that changed him from an adoring lover to a primitive being who seemed quite capable of murder.

'It must be embarrassing, naturally,' she owned, but there was no plea in her glance. 'I suppose she'll dislike me, and – and I can't blame her. It was very wrong and thoughtless of me to act in the way I did.'

This candid admission of guilt brought a flickering glance from Lean before, almost instantly, his face became impassive. But a movement at the side of his jaw gave her the impression that he was profoundly affected by her words.

'I don't think you need trouble yourself about her disliking you,' he said carelessly. 'It all happened so long ago that it's not important any more.'

Melanie swallowed hard, glancing past him to the open window through which the sun shone brilliantly from a sky of purest blue. Trees in the garden stood out in sharp relief against this backcloth of vaulted serenity – the carob, laden with shining green pods, the rounded shape of a lemon tree heavy with fruit yet at the same time displaying its sweetly-perfumed blossom, the jacaranda spreading its purple mist beside a vine-draped arbour from whose roof hung the grapes – huge unripe bunches covered with a soft grey bloom.

Lean was watching her, apparently awaiting some comment, and she found herself echoing his words, speaking softly and mechanically as if she were far away in the dim and distant past.

'Yes ... it all happened so long ago that it's not important any more....' She stopped and their eyes met across the desk. Not important any more ... so indifferent was his passing off of that. Why, then, this unswerving determination to be revenged on her?

CHAPTER SEVEN

'WHAT I can't understand,' said Sandra a few days later, 'is why, when he's so obviously grateful for what you did, he doesn't be a sport and let you off – oh, I don't mean he should waive the debt, but he could let you go back home and arrange for the money to be paid later. After all, it is your brother's debt.'

Melanie glanced out of the bus window. Two black-robed peasant women were coming up the rough brown track, ambling along beside their donkeys. They drew on to the field to allow the bus to pass. Automatically Melanie raised a hand in salute and the women smiled and responded with waves of their hands.

'I think it's better to be cleared off in this way,' she said at length. 'Gerard wouldn't ever be able to pay it.'

'You sound as if you don't want to go home.' The strange quality in Sandra's tone brought Melanie's head round. Her friend was looking most oddly at her.

'Naturally I want to return home, but I'd rather go when this debt's off my mind.' She had changed, of course, just as Sandra implied. Until the evening of Eleni's rescue the idea of returning to England just as soon as possible had been an obsession with Melanie . . . but now. . . .

Was it the change in Lean that had brought about her own resignation? Could it be that, because he happened to smile at her now and then, she was ready to forget his harsh treatment of her, to endure the humiliation which he still inflicted on her?

'You wouldn't be falling in love with him all over—?' Sandra stopped and amended with a grin, 'You wouldn't be falling in love with him, would you?'

'Certainly not!' Flushing hotly, Melanie returned her attention to the scene outside. The bus had stopped to allow some passengers to alight. Through an ornate wrought-iron gate she saw a paved courtyard, with a cascade of roses and hibiscus against a dazzling white wall, and the majestic figure of an aged woman, sitting on the step, a pestle and mortar on her knee. 'Lean Angeli is the last man I'd fall in love with!'

'All right, all right, I only asked.' But Sandra was still amused, even though she considerately changed the subject. 'I think it was a good idea of mine to suggest we come out here today. It's going to be really hot, so we'll be grateful for that lovely cool water.'

The beach at Mallia was of white sand backed by fields of olives, and banana plantations sheltered from the sea breezes by fences of high bamboos. It was a little early for the tourist masses and the girls had a lovely stretch of beach all to themselves. They swam, sunbathed, then swam again.

'I reckon I've made jolly good use of my first Wednesday off, thanks to your suggestion.' Melanie sat on the sand, her knees drawn up under her chin and her arms embracing them. 'This is much better than work.'

'I don't know how you've stuck it, working six days a week – and such long hours too. It would have knocked you up if you'd gone on.'

Melanie nodded. She had been feeling the strain and had herself wondered just how long she would have been able to go on like that. Certainly not for four years! She gazed out to sea and a frown settled on her brow. Had Lean really intended trying to prolong her punishment for that length of time? He was a practical, clear-thinking man and he must have realized the impossibility of her keeping up a pace like that for four years.

'It's time we dressed and went over to the café. The boys should be arriving any time now.'

Sandra had run into Giles the previous evening and told him of their intention of going to Mallia the following morning. He was working until twelve, but said he would be along and they would have lunch together at the café on the beach. He would bring Les, he promised, suggesting that they all go off somewhere in the afternoon.

The two men were waiting when they reached the café, partaking of iced drinks to the sound of Greek music – flutes and mandolines and a *bouzouki*.

'Hello there. Had a good swim?' Giles rose and fetched two more chairs. 'You're a lucky pair, having the whole day off.'

'You don't know how to do it,' laughed Sandra, taking a seat. 'Yes, we had a wonderful time in that water!'

'What are you drinking?' Les looked at Melanie, remembering, she had no doubt, the occasion of his first meeting with her. Had Giles given him any information regarding their activities on that evening? she wondered. She did not think so. Giles, she felt sure, was both tactful and trustworthy.

'Something long and cool,' she smiled, sitting down next to Giles and presently finding an opportunity of conveying Lean's thanks for his help.

'It was nothing,' he returned lightly. 'One would do it for any young girl in a plight like that.' They were speaking in lowered tones while the other two chatted, waiting for the drinks to be brought out to them.

'We wondered how you two would feel about a visit to St. Nikolaos? We can go on the bus.' Les paid for the

113

drinks as he spoke and the girls glanced at one another.

'I'd like it,' agreed Melanie. 'Is it far?' Vaguely it came to her that only a week ago she would not have spent even one drachma on pleasure, so precious was her money in the vital matter of acquiring her freedom at the earliest possible moment.

'Not far at all. It's a lovely run and there's a tropical lagoon where you can bathe – very romantic, isn't it, Giles?'

He nodded and laughed. It was agreed that they should have a snack lunch here at the beach café and then catch the bus for St. Nikolaos.

'What do we want to eat?' Sandra looked at her friend.

'A *meze*?' suggested Giles. 'For me, it'll be quite sufficient.'

The *meze* consisted of all sorts of vegetables; nuts, fish, cheese, olives, slices of tomatoes and rusk, all set out in separate dishes. Provided with forks, the four just picked where they liked, drinking *ouzo* with the *meze* and finishing off with fresh fruit salad and cream.

Melanie thoroughly enjoyed herself, for this of course was an unexpected treat. The tables were on the beach, shaded from the sun's heat and glare by the feathery tamarisk shrubs with their delicate sprays of creamy pink blossom. The sea was motionless and multicoloured in every shade from deepest green through turquoise and aquamarine to a vivid blue dappled here and there with golden tints stolen from the sun's rich store. In the opposite direction were the mountains, the limestone peaks of the Dhikti Range.

The road to St. Nikolaos climbed away from the coast, winding through a rocky and dramatic ravine. About half way through the ravine, standing on a ledge, was the monastery of Selinaris.

'We stop here,' Giles informed them even before the bus began to slow down. 'Everyone says a prayer for a safe journey through the mountain pass.'

The monks were sitting about under the oleanders, smoking cigarettes and watching the passengers alighting from the bus. Everyone went into the chapel, said their prayer, and then formed a queue to kiss the two ikons of St. George, the patron saint of the monastery. There were ikons of four other saints, a rather incongruous modern safe in which the offerings were kept, the usual brown candles found in every Greek Orthodox Church, and in addition, the less familiar *tassima*, those little models of the various parts of the body which people desired to be blessed – eyes and noses, heads, arms and legs, all of which were crowded round the altar.

Everyone piled into the bus and they were on their way again, winding and snaking and climbing through the craggy ravine. It was breathtaking, but also a rather frightening drive, and at every danger spot, where a dramatic precipice dropped sheer from the road, the Greek women would cross themselves and their lips would move in silent prayer.

'Scared?' Les was sitting with Melanie and his arm slid across the back of the seat.

'It is sort of – terrifying,' she admitted, not daring to look down, for her heart was already thumping most unnaturally. 'It's very beautiful, though.'

'Yes, the scenery is spectacular; and the air's so fresh and clear.'

'We're almost at the top,' Giles put in, leaning forward as he spoke. 'The descent isn't nearly so frightening.'

For some short distance the rugged aspect remained, and then the landscape became less dramatic. Several times the bus stopped, to pick up or drop mail-bags, crates of fruit or chickens. A couple of bicycles were duly delivered, along with various other commodities. At one village the bus stopped long enough for the passengers to alight and take refreshments at the road-side café.

'*Soumadha* is what one always drinks here,' Les said as he gave the order. 'Ever had it?'

'No.' Melanie shook her head. 'It's milky, isn't it, and made from almonds?'

'That's right. You'll like it.'

At St. Nikolaos they sat in the square for a while and then went down to the lagoon for a swim. But soon Melanie had had enough and she came out of the water and sat on the beach, gazing over the vast expanse of sea, her eyes occasionally settling on one or other of the swimmers out there. Presently Les joined her and they sat talking as they dried themselves in the sun. Les worked in a hotel, he told her. Like Giles and Sandra he was on the move, determined to see as much of the world as possible before taking a permanent post in England.

'Where are you bound for next?' Melanie asked interestedly.

'I haven't made up my mind. Turkey, perhaps, or Egypt, maybe. It's all open wide and I expect when the fit takes me to move on I'll simply toss a coin.' He paused, turning to examine her with a slightly puzzled expression on his handsome face. 'And you? Are you a roamer, too?'

'No; I intend working here for about two years; after that I'll be returning to England.'

Another pause, and then, hesitantly,

'What made you come to Crete?'

She turned her gaze seawards and a pensive look came into her eyes as they rested for a moment on the jagged outline of the massif which occupied a large area of the extreme eastern end of the island.

'The reason for my being here is private, Les,' she answered apologetically. 'I'm afraid I can't talk about it to anyone.' Her reply was accepted affably by Les and they resumed their casual conversation until the others eventually came out of the sea to join them.

Having all agreed to make a day of it they dined at a *taverna*, joined in the Greek dancing, and returned to Heraklion at half-past eleven. Lean had taken his mother and sister to visit friends and they had not yet returned, but Olga was on the verandah talking to one of the guests when Melanie and Les walked into the grounds of the hotel. Olga stopped talking and eyed them both for a moment and Melanie gained the impression that she was choosing her words carefully. However, her eyes suddenly glinted with a strange satisfaction and at the same time she spoke to her companion, having obviously changed her mind about any comment she had intended to make to Melanie.

The following morning Melanie once again found herself in her employer's office.

'I believe you know,' he began in harsh and frigid tones, 'that it is not permissible for the staff to bring their friends into those parts of the hotel and grounds used by the guests.'

She flushed with anger.

'Has Miss Newson nothing better to do than carry tales? My friend saw me home and went off immediately.'

'Went off immediately?' His fine brows shot up a fraction. 'That's not quite true, is it?'

She blinked at him.

'Certainly it's true. Les came to the entrance and then left me.'

'I think not.'

Melanie's eyes kindled.

'I don't know what Miss Newson has told you, but I'm speaking the truth when I say he left me immediately.'

'I believe you were – er – larking about with this man,' he said, ignoring her protest. 'You were both making some considerable noise which disturbed the guests. Now, it's none of my business what you do, but—'

Quiveringly Melanie cut him short by requesting that Olga be brought to the room. This naturally produced doubt, and Lean surprised Melanie by dropping his harsh manner and asking her to tell him exactly what had happened.

'There isn't anything to tell.' She met his gaze unflinchingly, distress mingling with the anger in her eyes. 'Les – this young man whom I've met only for the second time today – merely came with me as a courtesy gesture and, as I said, he went off immediately.' Giles and Sandra had been close behind, but Olga had not considered it necessary to inform Lean that Giles had also entered the hotel grounds. 'I'm telling the truth, Lean – Mr.—' She shook her head and to her amazement she surprised a flicker of emotion in his glance before he turned aside to become absorbed, it appeared, in a house lizard that had moved swiftly across the carpet in pursuit of a beetle that had unwisely flown into the room and alighted on the floor. It seemed imperative that he take her word and Melanie added in a faintly pleading tone, 'Do you . . . do you believe me?'

Losing interest in the activities of the lizard, Lean brought his gaze back to her, his eyes resting on her hands, clasped in front of her, the slight movement of her fingers betraying her suspense as to his reply.

His gaze shifted and for a long moment he regarded

her intently, his eyes boring into her as if he sought for the truth himself rather than accepting her word.

'Yes, Melanie,' he said at last. 'I believe you.'

She stared at him, wondering at the little sigh that had accompanied his words. For some incomprehensible reason she felt he actually *wanted* to believe her!

'Thank you,' she returned simply. 'Shall I go now?'

He merely nodded, in a vague and automatic way, his glance flicking to the lizard, which was now performing a most complicated dance as it twisted and turned in an endeavour to trap the beetle which was, for the present, managing successfully to evade each deadly thrust.

A little later, when Melanie was tidying out one of the bedrooms in the suite occupied by Eleni and her mother, Olga entered, an ugly gleam in her eyes. Swiftly she glanced around, then walked over to the window.

'When was this last cleaned?' she asked in a harsh and grating tone.

'I wasn't aware that window cleaning was included in my duties. I've never done them before.'

'With a private suite it's different. Get them cleaned; they're an absolute disgrace!'

Anger choked the retort that Melanie longed to make. She just stood there, while Olga found fault with everything she had done. The bed was not made right, the carpet must be swept again, and even the pretty ribbon holding back the curtains had not been tied to Olga's liking.

'You're quite sure that is all?' inquired Melanie at last. 'If so perhaps you'll leave me to get on with putting these matters right.' How she successfully controlled the fury that enveloped her Melanie never knew, but she did control it; the dignity of her voice and bearing seemed to release some pent-up emotion in the other girl and her eyes blazed with hatred as she said,

'What lies did you tell Lean this morning in order to induce him to accept your word in preference to mine?'

'The lies were yours,' Melanie replied quietly. 'I merely told him the truth. You were very foolish,' she went on to add, 'because it should have dawned on you that I would defend myself. On learning what you'd tried to do I asked that you be sent for.'

'Me? Sent for? You insolent creature! You seem to have forgotten who I am!'

Melanie gave an exasperated little sigh.

'Please go away. I'm already behind with my work.'

'I'll get even with you yet!' was Olga's snarling response. 'I don't know what's been going on that Lean should change towards you like this – it's ever since you and Eleni were out together, and it's obvious you've been fawning round Eleni and her mother, and that, through them, you're managing to ingratiate yourself with Lean—'

'Miss Newson!'

Both girls turned, to see Madam Angeli standing in the doorway, a look of amazement and disbelief on her dark and arrogant face. Tall, like Lean, she was possessed of a hauteur and commanding personality which had been passed on to her son along with her nobility of bearing and exceptional good looks.

'Madam Angeli!' Olga went grey. 'I – Melanie here, she's so – so slovenly and I'm having to – to . . .' Her voice faded as Olga recalled the last words Madam Angeli must have heard. 'She seems to have forgotten her place,' Olga added weakly in an effort to explain away those words.

'It appears that you also have forgotten your place, Miss Newson,' was Madam Angeli's frigid rejoinder. 'What makes you think your position allows you to treat your fellow human beings in this way? Is this demonstration typical of that to which all the staff here is subjected?'

'No – oh, no! It's just Melanie, because she's not only slipshod in her work, but insolent too.'

'Miss Newson,' said the older woman icily as she advanced into the middle of the room, 'I've been standing here for some time. I've listened to your deplorable treatment of Melanie, but I haven't heard one word of – insolence – as you call it, from her. On the contrary, she was far more restrained than I myself would have been in similar circumstances. Leave us, if you please – and you can expect to hear more about this later.'

The voice, so quietly commanding and impressive; the dark severity and depth of censure in the eyes; the hard compression of the mouth and inflexibility of the jaw ... all these brought to Melanie a startlingly clear image of her son. No timid subservient Greek wife this, but a woman who had deserted the ranks of vassalage to assert her rights and partake of the freedom enjoyed by the women of the West.

Olga went out, casting Melanie a venomous glance as she passed, a glance that sent an involuntary quiver of apprehension down Melanie's spine. There was no doubt in her mind that this girl would injure her if she could.

'Would you care to talk to me about it?' invited Madam Angeli as the door closed behind Olga Newson. 'In what way did you have to defend yourself this morning?'

Melanie hesitated, but there was an insistence about

Lean's mother that could not be ignored, and a moment later Melanie was relating to her all that had transpired a short while previously in Lean's office.

'She is not a nice person to be having in a place like this,' was Madam Angeli's comment as Melanie ended her narrative. 'Obviously she keeps this side of her nature from my son.' She paused musingly and then went on, 'Tell me, child, is she like this with all the staff?'

Melanie shook her head, making no attempt at evasion, for she at once concluded it would be useless.

'No, it's only with me.'

'Does she know you were once engaged to my son?'

A flush spread at this unexpected question.

'She doesn't know that, but she does know we're – we're not strangers.'

'She would like to marry Lean; you're aware of that, I suppose?' This rather intimate turn in the conversation embarrassed Melanie, but the older woman remained coolly unmoved as she went on to say that Olga was not the girl for her son and she would be both surprised and disappointed should he ever consider marriage to her. 'I haven't known you very long, Melanie,' she added, regarding her curiously from head to toe, 'but you're so different from what I expected that I feel there's much both Lean and I don't understand. Why did you agree to marry him and then give him up?'

The colour deepened in Melanie's cheeks and she lowered her eyes. She had not expected to be subjected to such forthright questioning as this.

'I've no excuse at all,' she confessed frankly. 'I was very young, and thoughtless – but that's not really an excuse.'

'But it is,' the older woman argued. 'We're all stupid

when we're young. Nature is most unkind to us; it gives us wisdom only when we have already made our mistakes. Would you do the same again?' And when Melanie shook her head, 'No, of course you wouldn't; you'd make sure of your feelings before entering into the contract. And what about this matter of the debt? Lean was so angry that I believe he didn't stop to think just what he was doing. The blame lay with your brother, I understand?'

'I had some of the money,' admitted Melanie, wishing fervently that she could escape from this woman's disconcerting presence. 'Also, Lean brought me here for quite another reason than the repayment of the money. You must be aware that he brought me here chiefly for vengeance. Eleni will have told you that?'

'She did. And I agree with her that my son must have loved you very deeply, otherwise he would never have harboured the desire for revenge all these years.' She regarded Melanie for a while in silence before reverting to her admission that she had received some of Eleni's money. 'It's a most puzzling circumstance,' she went on. 'You don't seem dishonest to me. Did you know the money was stolen?'

Melanie shifted uneasily, thinking of Gerard and experiencing a deep sense of guilt merely because he was her brother.

'I'd rather not talk about it,' she returned unsteadily. 'It's finished with, Madam Angeli – except for the repayment of the debt, that is.'

'You don't like being questioned? Well, that's understandable, so we'll let the matter drop. You can leave me now, Melanie, for I want to lie down for an hour or so. See to the room later – after lunch will do.'

CHAPTER EIGHT

IMMEDIATELY on finishing work that evening Melanie took a quick shower in Sandra's bathroom and went off to catch the bus that would take her to Androula's house. Having given her an hour's lesson Melanie refused the Greek girl's offer of supper and returned to the hotel. For she had had an especially tiring day and her only desire was to go to bed.

She took one step into her room and stopped. Perfume ... Olga's particular brand! Instinctively Melanie moved over to the recess in which her money was hidden behind the photograph of her parents. A little sigh broke from her lips as she took out the bundle of notes. All intact – but the new notes Kostagis had given her last Sunday were underneath, whereas Melanie had naturally placed them on top.

Was Olga aware that she received no salary? Melanie wondered, replacing her money in its hole in the wall and covering it with the photograph. Olga paid all the wages, so she must know there was something different where Melanie's money was concerned. It seemed feasible that she would ask Lean about this, and it seemed equally feasible that he would offer some explanation. If he had said he paid Melanie's salary into the bank then Olga would be wondering from what source this money had come, for it now amounted to twenty-four pounds.

With a deep frown settling on her brow Melanie glanced round the room, her eyes moving from the rugs on the floor to the attractive little chest of drawers serving as a dressing-table, and over which Sandra had placed the mirror. There was the comfortable easy chair, the attractive bed-cover. . . . Having been in Melanie's room on a previous occasion Olga knew exactly what should be here.

Melanie picked up the letter she had left lying on the chest of drawers and scanned the pages again. It was from Richard, with whom she had kept up a correspondence, though in a rather half-hearted way, for with every week that passed his image was becoming dimmer and she had known for some time that he could never hold any important place in her life. He was coming out for a holiday, he wrote, and he intended clearing up the mystery of her sudden departure for the island. 'I can't do without you either in my business or my private life,' he wrote. 'My only regret is that I didn't ask you to marry me long ago. However, that can soon be rectified, as you will see when I come out to Crete at the end of this month.' He had gone on to give her the date of his arrival, suggesting she book him in at the Hotel Avra.

Had Olga read this letter? But of course she had. Melanie could not imagine the girl's being so honourable as to refrain from picking it up.

Somehow the knowledge that Olga had been up here, had seen the changed room and knew of the little hoard in the wall, unsettled Melanie and, sure that sleep would be denied her, she went down to see if Sandra had returned from her visit to some Greek friends she had recently made, but the apartment was empty. Too restless to sit and read or even listen to her friend's radio, Melanie went downstairs and out to that part of the garden reserved for the staff.

The moon was waning, but it was a lovely starlit night, warm and balmy with a breeze coming in from the sea. Melanie sat down on one of the chairs and thought about Olga's visit to her room. What object could the girl have? She had spoken only that morning of 'getting even' with Melanie. Could it be, then, that her prying this evening had been conducted in the hope of finding something she could report to Lean? If so then fate had certainly been with her, and Melanie felt a tinge of foreboding at the prospect of being confronted with Lean and having to offer him some explanation both about the room and the money.

From across the way came the lively strains of *bouzouki* music, and Melanie could imagine the group of men, arm in arm and shoulder to shoulder, performing the intricate *pentozali*, the dance in which the men exhibited both their gracefulness and bodily strength, for the *pentozali* was the traditional Cretan fighters' dance.

Melanie's attention was brought from the music to sounds closer to. Footsteps on the terrace on the other side of the high screen of oleanders; they stopped and Melanie looked up to see Lean peering over the hedge. She was in the shadows and all he saw was a dark and indistinct silhouette.

'Melanie? It is Melanie, isn't it?'

'Yes.' Her pulse fluttered as he came round to the gate and entered the garden. Had he seen Olga? Did he know already about the change in her room, and the money?

'May I join you?'

His words took her completely by surprise and she said in some confusion,

'Yes, of c-course.'

He sat down, facing the lights on the front of the hotel. Melanie looked steadily at him and came to the conclusion that he had not yet learned anything from Olga Newson.

'My mother's told me what happened this morning,' he began without preamble. 'I've had a word with Miss Newson about it, and I don't think she'll trouble you like that again.' His voice was cool, impersonal, containing no hint of apology. Melanie examined his features – classical Greek features, noble, flint-like, with a hidden vigour which the famous sculptors of old so cleverly and subtly brought out in their images of the mythical gods of Olympus.

Melanie made no comment on what Lean had said and as the moments passed she became more and more uncomfortable in his presence. It seemed so odd that he should come and sit with her, in this small area of the garden reserved for his staff. True, he had been very different towards her since the night of his sister's grim adventure, but he still regarded her as an employee – a menial, as he had once so disparagingly termed her.

'I think I'll go in now,' she said awkwardly. 'I just came down for a breath of fresh air before I went to bed.'

'I've intruded,' he returned, and there was now a hint of apology in his voice. 'Perhaps you'd rather be alone?'

She stared, amazed by the question. Did he want to stay with her? Surely that was not possible . . . and yet why was he here at all?

As if to add to her turmoil of mind the years slipped away and she was in Lean's arms, scared yet excited by his lovemaking. With a sudden shock it came to her that he was the only man to whom she had ever visualized surrendering her body, that her fears had stemmed from the possibility of his tempting her . . . and her being quite unable to resist him. But always he had been honourable. She had not known then that, should a Greek ever indulge in an affair, it would never be with his intended wife, for by tradition a Greek girl must be pure on marriage, and this would apply to any girl whom he might choose for a wife.

'No, you haven't intruded. I – I don't—' She

stopped, blushing furiously at the idea that she was going to say she didn't want him to go.

Lean turned his head to look straight into her eyes. He smiled faintly at her confusion and she did begin to wonder if he were trying to read her thoughts, so intently was his gaze fixed upon her.

'Yes – you don't . . . ?'

'I meant you needn't go.'

The air seemed electrified; it was the tensest moment Melanie had ever known, for as she sat there, under a starlit Eastern sky, and with the scented breeze on her face, she at last allowed the truth to penetrate the barrier she had deliberately erected against it.

What a fool she had been to throw him over! Yes, she now freely admitted it, admitted the truth of what Sandra had said.

Seven years. She could have been Lean's wife for the past seven years. They would have had a family by now— She stopped. Impossible to assess the extent of her loss; unprofitable to dwell upon it. Nature was unkind to us, Madam Angeli had said. It gave us wisdom only when we had already made our mistakes.

'I needn't go.' Lean's softly spoken repetition of her words seemed only to add to the tension and she stirred restlessly. 'You want me to stay?'

She shook her head, unable to speak. The *bouzouki* music became louder; song and laughter mingled with it, and nearer to, the cicadas' incessant chirping floated out from the trees in which they were hidden. The breeze still blew in from the sea, capturing perfume as it advanced across the flower-strewn gardens. The sea itself was no longer a wide expanse of translucent turquoise, but merely a vague and darkened blur coalescing indistinctly with the sky.

It suddenly dawned on Melanie that Lean was waiting for an answer to his question. She wanted him to stay . . . more than anything she wanted that, but naturally she could not tell him so. The moments passed; she became increasingly unsure of herself and at last she rose unsteadily to her feet.

'I must go in,' she said. 'It's very late.'

He merely nodded, and stood up, for a moment entering into the shadows. It was impossible to see his face, but she had the extraordinary impression that he was disappointed by her decision to go indoors.

'I expect you're tired.' He moved with her as she made her way slowly to the little wrought-iron gate that separated the staff garden from the grounds proper. 'Melanie, about your hours — you'll have the same hours as Sandra from now on. I'll arrrange for a relief for you.'

'You're shortening my hours?' She stopped abruptly and looked up at him, her eyes wide and searching. 'Is it because of — of Eleni?'

'Because of your rescuing her?' He deliberately glanced away, avoiding her gaze. 'No,' he said, 'it's not because of Eleni.'

'Then why . . . ?' she asked quiveringly, and because all her attention was with her companion the fact that a totally different perfume floated on the air did not register until some time later.

'Both Mother and Eleni consider me to be too harsh with you,' came the surprising admission. 'They feel there is much I don't know.'

They had both been busy on her behalf then . . . and with some success, apparently.

'About the money?'

Returning his gaze to her, he asked if she had known the money was stolen from his sister. She answered truthfully and felt a quickening of her pulse as a deep sigh left his lips.

'So — in the case of Eleni, at least — you were not

guilty of any theft— Or rather, I should say, you did not knowingly receive stolen money.' A statement, and because it conveyed the fact that he believed her she returned impulsively,

'Mrs. Skonson's earrings, Lean, I didn't touch them – I swear it.'

They were standing very close, near the gate. Everything but the tiny garden seemed to be shut out, lost in a timelessness that affected them both.

'You said you'd do anything to find the money, so that you could get away from here,' he reminded her, yet with a strange mingling of doubt and expectancy.

'I wouldn't steal to get it,' she responded in grave and candid tones. 'At that time I was desperate to get away and I said the first thing that came into my head. But I wouldn't steal,' she reasserted firmly. He did not speak and something made her add, 'Did you really believe I'd stolen them?' She watched him closely, for somehow it now struck her that he had always had his doubts.

'I don't know, Melanie,' he admitted at length. 'You had no money, because of course I'm not paying you anything, and I suppose it seemed feasible that you had taken—' He stopped abruptly, shaking his head. 'No, I couldn't really accept the fact that you'd stolen them.'

'So you believe me – that I didn't touch them?'

'Yes,' he returned, a strange note of gruffness in his tone. 'I don't know why Olga should have tried to blacken your name like that – but yes, I do believe you, Melanie.'

'Oh ... *thank* you!' she breathed, and a softness touched the corners of his mouth, a softness that brought another fleeting vision of the past to increase the yearning that had already entered into her.

They stood for a long while, but Melanie was by now so afraid of revealing her emotions that she again announced her intention of going indoors. Suiting action to her words, she turned suddenly, forgetting the gate was closed. On a sort of rebound she fell against him; and before either had quite realized it she was in his arms and his lips sought hers in a kiss which seemed to release some long-forgotten, pent-up ardour, and Melanie was breathless when at last he held her from him.

'Must I apologize?' he inquired in a faintly mocking tone.

Dumbly she shook her head. What had she expected? A declaration of love? His dark eyes reflected the mockery of his tones and, twisting from his embrace, she opened the gate and ran through the grounds to the back entrance of the hotel.

A few moments later, quivering with disappointment, Melanie was in her tiny apartment. And it was only then, on becoming aware of the perfume, still hanging in the airless room, that she recalled that perfume in the garden . . .

Sandra gave a little start of surprise on hearing of the alteration to Melanie's hours, and murmured almost to herself,

'I wonder what the next move will be?' They were in her room, having coffee during the morning break. 'Wednesday off, and now your hours cut . . . things begin to look interesting.'

The verandah door was open; Melanie looked away, over the harbour to the blue Aegean, gleaming beneath a cloudless sky. Her expression was wistful, and faintly puzzled. Lean must have wanted to be with her last evening . . . he must in fact have wanted to kiss her, otherwise he would not have done so. And yet he had then adopted that air of mockery, appearing to be merely amused by the incident.

'In what way, interesting?' she asked with feigned lack of comprehension.

Sandra flicked her an amused, perceptive glance.

'You're not denying the situation's changed, I hope?'

'I suppose it would be useless to do so,' Melanie was forced to admit.

'He's obviously worried about you – about your health, probably – and that can mean only one thing, Melanie.'

'Lean will never fall in love with me again, if that's what you're thinking.'

'No, that's not what I'm thinking,' returned Sandra on a cryptic note. 'Odd, isn't it, that neither of you has ever married?'

Melanie's eyes flickered. Already she had been struck by that circumstance, dwelling on it often since that first vague awareness of her feelings for the man to whom she had once been engaged.

After throwing Lean over she had devoted all her time and energy to the realization of her ambition. Having achieved that ambition she had become totally absorbed in making a success of her job, and so the years had slipped by, and it was only when Richard had begun to take a personal interest in her that she had allowed the idea of marriage to intrude into her life. But even then, she had followed no smooth and direct course with that prospect as her goal. Her way with Richard had been halting, barred by uncertainty and indecision, and Melanie now knew for sure that even had she not met Lean again, she would never have married Richard.

'Lean's probably been fully occupied with his business,' she offered, not very convincingly. 'He has several hotels on the island, as you know, but I seem to remember that he inherited hotels and property in other parts of Greece.'

'Yes, I expect he has been occupied with his business, but there must still have been time to search around for a wife ... should he have desired to have one.' Sandra emptied her cup and put it on the tray. 'And you ... have you never had anyone else?'

'Richard,' said Melanie absently.

'Richard? Who's he?'

'The man I worked for. He's coming here for a holiday in about two weeks' time.'

'Your boss?' Sandra eyed her in surprise. 'You never said there was anything else in your relationship?'

'I once thought I might marry him.'

'I see ... and now?' Sandra cast her a sideways glance and waited interestedly for her response.

'I'll never marry Richard,' she said simply, taking a glance at the clock, and discovering to her relief that their coffee break was at an end. For it was evident that, given the opportunity, Sandra would pursue the subject much too far for Melanie's comfort.

Eleni was sitting at the dressing-table, varnishing her nails when Melanie went in to make the beds.

'I'll come back later,' she began, but Eleni interrupted her.

'No, don't go, Melanie. I've something to talk to you about. Sit down.' Her manner was one of eagerness, but there was also something of the conspirator about her movements as she laid aside the bottle of varnish and swivelled round on her stool. Melanie took possession of the chair by the bed and waited in some perplexity for what was to come. Eleni did not waste words and within seconds Melanie's face was scarlet as she stammered,

'How d-do you know Lean k-kissed me?'

'I've been listening at the door,' admitted the Greek girl blandly. 'Do you want to know everything I heard?'

'You've listened . . . ?'

'Don't be shocked, Melanie. I couldn't really help it. You see, I went in to Lean – through the little room at the back of his office; you know, the one that you can enter from a verandah?'

'I haven't seen it.'

'No? Well, it's a small room Lean uses as a sort of store place for books and ledgers and the like. As I said, I went in that way and immediately realized Lean and Olga were talking in the outer office, so I stayed where I was. At first I couldn't tell what it was all about, but it soon became clear that Olga had let slip something which gave Lean a clue that she'd been spying on you two last evenings in the garden. Lean was very angry, for she kept denying it. But then she admitted it and began talking about all she had overheard.' A little silence, and then, 'She asked him why he was kissing you.' Melanie's eyelids fluttered. Olga had witnessed the kissing incident . . . Had she also heard the mockery in Lean's tones a moment later when asking if he should apologize? 'From her tones I deduced that Olga was having difficulty in keeping her temper,' continued Eleni, 'but she did manage it, and spoke quietly enough. It seemed obvious that she expected Lean to marry her one day, and I'm sure there's something between them. Do you think she's his pillow friend?'

Melanie's colour heightened.

'I w-wouldn't know,' she said in some confusion.

Eleni gestured with her hands as if making an affirmative answer to her own question.

'She's obviously intimate enough with him to be able to speak her mind. She even asked him outright if you and he had had an affiair in England.'

'She did!' Melanie stared in disbelief. Yes, there must be something between them for Olga to dare ask a question like that. 'What did he say?'

'Told her it was none of her business. And he was so frigid with her – you know how he can be when he's in one of his superior moods. I'm sure Olga was feeling most uncomfortable.' Picking up the varnish bottle, Eleni regarded the label in an absent sort of way. 'Is Lean in love with you again?' she asked, right out of the blue.

'No, of course he isn't!'

'But he kissed you . . .?'

'It was an accident. . . .' That sounded rather silly and Melanie went on to explain what had happened. 'It didn't mean a thing,' she asserted with a lightness she hoped sounded convincing.

'Lean isn't a flirt,' submitted his sister without much expression. Melanie did not comment and Eleni went on to repeat all she had overheard. It was soon clear that Olga had been on the other side of that hedge the whole time, listening to everything that had passed between Lean and Melanie. She had commented on his reducing Melanie's hours and had even brought up the matter of Mrs. Skonson's earrings. As Eleni had not previously heard the story she was in the dark and Melanie felt obliged to give her a brief account of what had occurred. Eleni's eyes darkened angrily at the idea of Melanie's being wrongly accused of theft.

'They had a big argument over it,' she went on. 'Olga said you'd definitely stolen the earrings.'

A hint of fear darkened Melanie's eyes as she asked,

'Did her words appear to have any effect? I mean, did Lean seem to believe her?'

Eleni shook her head.

'He said he should have investigated more

thoroughly at the time; he told her he was no longer satisfied with her story. He believed she'd lied and demanded an explanation as to why she had done it.'

'And then?'

'She wouldn't admit anything, still maintaining you'd stolen them and that she found them in your room.'

Melanie swallowed hard. Would this firm denial give rise to renewed doubts in Lean's mind?

'How did it end?'

'Lean was impatient and said to let the matter drop. But then he warned her she would have to be different with the staff, and that with you ... well, she must treat you with more respect. I was so glad, for I just hate that girl and can't imagine what Lean sees in her. ... It could be that his only interest in her is from a business angle, though, for she is terribly efficient,' Eleni grudgingly conceded as an afterthought before continuing, 'There was a big silence and I wondered if Olga was crying. However, she wasn't, because she changed the subject, telling Lean some furniture and other things were missing. She even hinted that they'd been stolen – which was ridiculous!' Melanie's long lashes came down, hiding her expression.

'What did Lean say to that?'

'He sounded so impatient again, and fairly snapped at her, saying it was her affair and not to bring such minor matters to his notice. She then said something about having the whole place searched, and he just said, in the same snappy tones, "Please yourself, but don't trouble me with it!" I didn't stay to hear any more but left the way I had entered.'

Olga did trouble him with it and as Melanie expected she was summoned into his presence even yet again. This time, however, he asked that she come to his sitting-room after dinner, as he was paying a periodic visit to one of the hotels on the south coast and would not be back at the Hotel Avra until nine o'clock.

Melanie knocked on his door at ten minutes past; Lean opened it himself and bade her enter. A flush tinted her cheeks as she glanced up at him, but if he too were remembering that kiss his expression gave no evidence of it. To Melanie's relief he was alone; she had convinced herself that Olga would be a witness when Lean demanded an explanation.

To her surprise his voice held neither anger nor accusation as he asked her to take a seat.

'Thank you.' She sat on the couch, on the very edge, for she could not relax until she had gleaned some idea of the outcome of this interview.

'Can I offer you a drink?' He stood over her, immaculate in a dark grey lounge suit and with a gleaming white shirt throwing into relief the rich deep bronze of his skin. 'Sherry?'

'Thank you,' she said again, bewildered by this reception.

Lean poured the drinks, handed Melanie hers and then brought up a small inlaid table for her to put it on. He opened a silver cigarette box, but she shook her head. Lean took out a cigarette and lighted it; she had never before seen him smoke, she reflected, and thought it must be only on rare occasions that he had a cigarette.

'Did Olga tell you what I wanted to see you about?' he asked, taking a seat opposite to her.

'Yes. I know why you've sent for me.'

Lean drew on his cigarette; he watched her face, taking in the fluctuating colour, the tremor of her mouth and the anxiety in her soft brown eyes.

'What have you to say about removing these things to your room, Melanie?'

'It's so difficult,' she began, having no idea how she

would explain. 'The room – was so uncomfortable, and—'

'It was meant to be uncomfortable, you were fully aware of that.'

She nodded helplessly.

'Yes. . . .' Placing her glass on the table, Melanie took a cigarette from the box. Reaching across, Lean gave her a light. 'I'm sorry,' she murmured when he had to make several attempts. She hadn't realized she trembled so.

'You took some of the things from guest rooms, I believe?'

She tried to think.

'Oh, yes,' she agreed brightly. 'I've an idea the chair came from . . .' Melanie tailed off as Lean's eyes opened wide in an interrogative stare. 'Yes, it did – I mean, I took it from one of the guest rooms.'

A silver ash tray lay on the table; Lean flicked his ash into it and said softly,

'Which room was that?'

'Er – now let me think. . . . One of those on the first floor. . . .' Had he been up and taken a look at her room? She thought not, but couldn't be sure. Her chair was upholstered in blue; those on the first floor were in gold. 'No – it was one of the rooms on the third floor.'

'One of those on the third floor?' Lifting his glass, he took a drink. 'May I have now the truth?' he requested softly.

'The . . . truth?'

'If you please.'

'I've just said, I took the chair from one of the guest rooms.'

Lean uttered an exasperated sigh and put down his glass.

'Where did you get the other things?'

Melanie gave a careless little shrug.

'They were about somewhere. Things are all over the place.'

'They are?' His brows rose slightly. 'That's news to me.'

Melanie bit her lip. Only now did it dawn on her that Lean knew she was lying. She blinked at him, the smoke hurting her eyes as she absently held the cigarette right under her face.

'Perhaps you'd better put that out,' he suggested, at the same time taking it from her and stubbing it in the ash tray. 'Who got you the things?'

She shook her head.

'I'd rather not say.'

'Which is both natural and commendable,' he returned, amazing her by the cool and matter-of-fact way he accepted that. 'It's of no importance, anyway.'

'You don't mind?' she gasped.

'I would have done had the matter been brought to my notice earlier, but not now – not since my indebtedness to you over Eleni.'

'Indebtedness?' she repeated flatly. 'Is that the only reason you're not annoyed—?' She broke off, lowering her head. What a thing to say!

'Was there some other reason you were thinking of?' he inquired, in soft and even tones.

Dejectedly she shook her head.

'Of course not.' But even as she spoke something struck her. If he hadn't sent for her in order to reprimand her, then why had he sent for her at all?

Lean regarded her for a moment, then his gaze fell to her empty glass on the table.

'Another drink?'

Melanie found him baffling, and as she herself felt awkward she refused the drink and said that if he had nothing more to say to her she would leave him.

'I usually go for a walk in the evening,' she added by way of explanation, even while realizing an explanation was quite unnecessary.

'Then I won't keep you.' Lean rose, and the fact that he had no intention of pressing her to remain filled Melanie with disappointment. Why was she here at all? she asked herself again. And why, having been invited to stay and have another drink with Lean, had she foolishly refused, cutting short these moments which, despite her awkwardness and the tumult within her, she desperately wanted to prolong?

CHAPTER NINE

WHILE cool politeness still marked Lean's attitude towards Melanie, a subtle change was taking place. Gradually penetrating the veil of apparent indifference was a hint of warmth which, when manifested either by a smile or friendly word, would involve Melanie in a disturbing restlessness mingled with regret. If only their paths had crossed later . . .

Occasionally in his manner she would detect a restraint, as if he were holding in check some strong desire. At these times Melanie would become acutely alive to Sandra's subtle prophecies of a reconciliation, but almost at once hope would die. Tolerance – and perhaps friendliness – Lean might eventually exhibit towards her . . . forgiveness for that past slight and hurt, never.

But although he himself appeared to be intent on keeping her at arm's length, Lean had no control over the friendship that was rapidly developing between his sister and his ex-fiancée. Madam Angeli too was becoming extremely fond of Melanie, and this resulted in her inviting Melanie to accompany Eleni and herself on a trip to the south of the island. In addition to the hotels owned by Lean, Madam Angeli and her son jointly owned others, and it was her practice to display interest by a periodic visit to these hotels when she would interview the managers and ascertain for herself the efficiency with which they were being run. It was planned that they go off early the following Wednesday morning, returning on the Thursday evening. Melanie thanked Madam Angeli profusely for her invitation, but pointed out that she would not be free on

Thursday. To her astonishment it had already been arranged that she should have the extra day off work.

The news spread swiftly, but many of the staff were not interested. Sandra, however, received the information with a rather expressionless,

'Well, well, now just fancy that . . .'

Olga's reaction was to intensify her fault-finding with Melanie's work, despite Lean's order that she treat her with more respect.

She must thank Lean, Melanie decided, and this she did, having opportunely met him in the corridor.

'It's nothing,' he returned coolly. 'Eleni has taken a liking to you and it will be nice for her to have your company on the trip.' An unexpected smile came to his lips; Melanie gave a little silent intake of her breath. It did nothing for her peace of mind to see that smile. She was just moving away when he spoke; she turned, looking up at him expectantly, her soft lips quivering slightly, an outward sign of the unrest within. 'Melanie. . . .' For a brief space he seemed hesitant, and as she waited she sensed an oppression about him, as if he were burdened in some way. 'As you know, the new girl left last week-end. You can take over her room.'

'I can – move?' She stared in disbelief, stunned by this concession. 'Thank you . . . thank you very much.' Collecting herself, she gave him a glowing glance; his smile appeared again, but before he had time to speak Olga came round the corner and almost bumped into them. Nothing was lost on her and her eyes narrowed as they moved from Lean's smiling countenance to Melanie's glowing face.

'Olga,' said Lean immediately, 'my mother wants some money. Get her about three thousand drachmae, will you?'

'Does she require it now?'

'She wants it for Wednesday— No, Tuesday evening, as they're setting off very early on Wednesday.'

Olga cast a dark malignant glance at Melanie, and then passed on, disappearing round the corner at the other end of the corridor.

'I hope you'll enjoy the trip,' he said, turning to Melanie and smiling down at her. And then, as if reaching a sudden decision, 'I've a good mind to come along myself ... yes, I haven't visited the Palladian since the new manager took over.'

Eleni and her mother were delighted at the idea of Lean's accompanying them, and it warmed Melanie's heart to see the affection existing in this family. She thought of her own family; they too had been united until that escapade of Gerard's which had produced a rift between him and Melanie that threatened to be lasting. She had received a letter from her mother two days ago, saying that Gerard was still unemployed, yet he did not appear to be short of money. It was all very distressing, and Melanie had written to her brother urging him to find work, and also to drop the undesirable associates with whom he was obviously still mixing. 'Father is ill,' she added, 'and his anxiety over you isn't helping his condition.'

On the Monday evening prior to the trip Melanie and Sandra were in Melanie's new room, scrubbing and polishing, for it had not been left in a very clean condition.

'I suppose the thing would have been to leave it until I come back,' said Melanie with a little selfconscious laugh. 'But I can't wait to get settled in.'

'You're much happier than when you first came,' observed Sandra, looking up. She was on her knees in the tiny kitchen, scrubbing away at the attractively tiled floor. 'The boss is certainly intending to make your life easier.' She bent over the floor again and

Melanie continued with her task of pressing the curtains she had washed during her coffee break that morning.

'Let me come in here now,' she offered, having finished her ironing. 'I'm not letting you do all the dirty jobs.'

'I've done it the wrong way round,' laughed Sandra. 'I should have cleaned out the cupboard first, but these tiles do look so nice when they've been scrubbed that I just had to get at them.'

She rose as she spoke; the floor was finished and Sandra regarded it with pleasure and pride. She took the bucket downstairs to empty it and Melanie stepped carefully across to the cupboard.

A few minutes later Sandra returned, having left the bucket in the kitchen. She was quiet and Melanie glanced through the doorway, to see her busily polishing a chair. The outer door was open and suddenly Olga appeared, her expression one of arrogant surprise as she stopped, her eyes moved past Sandra to where Melanie was standing in the doorway.

'What's going on here?' she demanded, her voice sharp to the point of harshness. 'What are you two girls doing in this room?'

'Melanie's moving in.' Sandra flicked her cloth at an imaginary speck of dust on the sideboard. 'We're giving it a good spring-clean; it certainly needs it.'

Olga's handsome features took on an ugly twist. Brushing unceremoniously past Sandra, she came face to face with Melanie.

'Mr. Angeli's given you permission to take over this apartment?'

Melanie nodded and went back to her task of cleaning out the cupboard. Olga followed, softly closing the door behind her.

'Do you want something?' inquired Melanie in surprise, and Olga's mouth compressed.

'It appears you're being greatly favoured.'

'The English staff usually have these rooms,' Melanie reminded her. 'There's nothing unusual in my occupying one of them.'

'Then why weren't you occupying one at first?'

Melanie glanced up sharply, inclined to ask her to leave, yet somehow unable to do so, realizing to her surprise that she was pitying the girl. There was a greyness about Olga's face; Melanie recalled that previous loss of control and wondered if she were about to witness another display of Olga's temper.

'The reason for my being up there is not your concern—'

'But yours and Lean's – is that what you're going to say?'

'Well . . . yes.'

Olga's teeth snapped together; she moved closer to Melanie.

'I wish you'd never come here,' she snarled. 'What was there between you? You've had a love affair, haven't you? – and for some reason you parted!' The colour left Melanie's face, but she remained silent. Should she order Olga out? Sandra was in the other room; there might be a scene . . .

'I refuse to answer that,' she said quietly at last.

'He was in England many years ago – he told me that. It must have been then that you met. There was something between you; there's a reason for your coming here, tolerating what you have tolerated. And your money? You don't get paid—'

'How do you know that?' Melanie's tones quivered with anger and a sparkle entered her eyes.

'I happened to overhear Lean say something to you about it.'

'Ah . . . yes. You listened to us when we were in the

145

garden.' Melanie stopped, but it was too late. She had said enough to make Olga ask how she knew of the eavesdropping.

'It's not important,' replied Melanie evasively, but Olga was now shaking with fury.

'Lean! He's told you – oh, how hateful of him to discuss me with you – you, no more than a servant here – and me the manageress. I hate you both!' She spoke wildly, her face crimson with anger. 'Who are you, to be treated as an equal by the Angelis? A room maid to be going on a trip with Lean and his family! I can't think what's come over him! Why is he doing it?'

So she knew about the coming trip. Had Lean told her? Melanie rather thought it would have been Eleni who enlightened her.

'I can't discuss Lean's actions with you, Olga.' Melanie spoke quietly, still feeling sorry for the girl, despite her open hostility. 'You talk of my being a room maid – talk in a disparaging sort of way, and in fact I am a room maid and nothing more. But in England I had a position quite equal to yours.' It was a much higher position, commanding a far greater salary, Melanie felt sure, but of course she did not say that. 'I don't consider myself inferior to Lean and his family.'

A sneer increased the already ugly curve of the older girl's mouth.

'You've had an exaggerated opinion of yourself since the moment of coming here,' she snapped, succeeding in bringing to Melanie's mind the occasion of that first meeting – the clash – with this girl. 'What you need is bringing down, and I shall—'

'Can I come in?' Sandra's swift glance spoke volumes as it flickered to Melanie, standing there, with her back to the sink, the scrubbing brush in her hand. 'I want some water, Melanie, and a wash leather. The windows are thick with dust.'

'Thank you,' breathed Melanie as the door slammed behind Olga. 'I was beginning to consider ordering her out.'

'Was she especially objectionable?'

A faint smile at that. Olga was always objectionable, she told her friend, before, dipping the brush into the warm soapy water, she resumed her task of cleaning out the cupboard.

But her pleasure in the preparation of the flat had faded, for all she could think about was Olga's final words, 'What you need is bringing down, and I shall—' Relieved as Melanie was by the entrance of her friend, she did wish she could have heard the end of Olga's sentence. It contained a threat, Melanie felt certain, and although she kept trying to reassure herself that there was no way in which Olga could harm her, she was all the while conscious of a tinge of uneasiness.

Gradually, however, she managed to throw off her fears, and excitement entered into her both at the idea of moving to the delightful little apartment and also at the prospect of the visit to the south of the island with Madam Angeli and her daughter . . . and Lean.

But little did she know as she continued to work enthusiastically, humming to herself as she dusted and polished and moved the furniture around, that she was destined neither to take possession of the tiny 'flat' nor accompany Lean and his family on the trip. For later, while fixing the curtains, she twisted round on hearing footsteps at her door, and her heart seemed to jerk right into her throat as she saw the expressions of her visitors. On Olga's face was a look of undisguised triumph, while Lean's jaw was rigid, his mouth set and his eyes hard and cold. And yet, as she came down off the stool and stood there, waiting, almost choked by palpitation, she realized with a little sense of shock that there were tiny grey lines at the corners of Lean's mouth and a sort of bewildered disbelief mingling with the metallic expression in his eyes.

'Melanie—' He stopped, as if having difficulty in framing his sentence. 'Mother's lost some money — from her handbag.'

'Lost?' she echoed uncomprehendingly, even while her heart continued to race with almost sickening speed. 'I – I don't understand?'

Lean opened his mouth and then closed it again, shaking his head. He appeared to be oblivious of Olga's presence when at last he managed to say,

'There's some mistake – there must be. You surely wouldn't take—' The words seemed to stick in his throat. Melanie watched, fascinated by the pulsating muscle at the side of his jaw. Olga threw him a faintly contemptuous glance and said without hesitation,

'Madam Angeli has had some money stolen from her handbag. As you know, I saw you with her bag and asked what you were doing—'

'You—!' Melanie stared in blank bewilderment, the colour draining from her face. 'What d-did you s-say?'

Olga shrugged impatiently.

'I hope you're not going to deny it.' She looked straight at Melanie, and not even by the flicker of an eyelid was any sign of shame or guilt portrayed. 'You instantly pushed the bag in a drawer and said you were merely tidying up the room.'

Melanie gasped. Despite all this girl had done to her, despite the fears resulting from that unfinished threat, Melanie could not at first take in these malicious lies and she just stood there, regarding her enemy in stupefaction. For a long while she held Olga's gaze before the older girl tilted her head and looked away. It was an arrogant gesture, making no impression on Lean or causing him to regard Olga with any sign of dawning suspicion.

'You saw me tampering with Madam Angeli's handbag? You're saying you actually *saw* me!'

Olga's sigh could be heard in the silence following Melanie's incredulous exclamation.

'I suppose it's natural that you should deny it – or rather, try to brazen it out. But this pretence wastes time . . .'

'Melanie . . .' Lean's soft voice cut short Olga's words, 'have you any explanation? Did you tamper with my mother's handbag?'

Melanie shook her head.

'No. . . .' She took a faltering step towards him, extending a hand in desperate entreaty. 'I haven't touched it. Please believe me – I wouldn't steal from your mother – or anyone. These are lies, and both she and I know they are . . . but you . . .? You have only my word.' She swallowed something in her throat, feeling choked by fear and emotion, for hope was fast deserting her. 'I haven't taken the money,' she repeated, and now even her lips had lost their colour. 'I wouldn't steal – I couldn't.'

Despairingly she thought, 'I seem always to be standing before him, accused of something I haven't done.'

It was a tense moment; Lean looked inquiringly at Olga.

'You've heard what Melanie has to say? Perhaps you'll explain?'

'Denials are to be expected. But we both know, Lean, that I saw her with your mother's bag. The only thing to do is search her room.'

A shuddering sigh broke from Melanie's lips. She saw it all now, saw the whole picture emerging. Bitterly she regretted not having informed Olga of the discovery that she had been in her room, and handled her money. That might have deterred her from an action such as this. But she could not mention it now, for she realized only too well that it would appear to have been thought up on the spur of the moment, in order to weaken Olga's accusation. Besides, Lean would want to know where she had obtained the money, and this she dared not say.

'How much was ... lost?' Melanie inquired, even while she knew the answer.

'The sum missing is seventeen hundred drachmae.'

So Olga had counted it, and taken the exact amount from Madam Angeli's bag. She looked up at Lean, with a frank, clear gaze, but even as she did so she felt the tears prick the backs of her eyes and to her dismay, they fell on to her cheeks. Flicking them away, she turned her attention to Olga; her voice was stiff and cold when she spoke.

'You're saying that when you saw me tampering with Madam Angeli's bag I was in fact stealing her money?'

'Madam Angeli has just reported the theft, and I instantly recalled what I'd seen. I'm not saying you have the money—' She broke off, shrugging. 'I can't say that, can I? But I do know that you were handling the bag when I passed the room.'

'I was robbing Madam Angeli ... with the door wide open for anyone to see ...?'

Lean glanced sharply at her, and then his eyes flickered to Olga. Again she did not move a muscle that would give the least evidence of her guilt.

'I've suggested searching Melanie's room. It seems the most sensible thing to do.'

Another trembling sigh left Melanie's lips. They would go to her room ... and find the exact amount. ... She looked at Lean, tears again in her eyes.

'How can I convince you?' she quivered. 'How can I make you believe I'm not a thief?'

'By letting us search your room, Melanie,' came Lean's quiet and practical reply. 'I'm requesting this most reluctantly, but one of you is lying and I must obviously do my best to find out which it is.' The hard set lines had gone; his glance seemed almost tender. 'You do understand, don't you?'

Melanie lowered her head. Through the open window floated the strains of *bouzouki* music from the taverna across the street. The sound, usually enjoyed by Melanie, now grated on her ears.

Her mouth felt parched, and she drew a trembling hand across her forehead, faintly surprised at finding beads of perspiration there.

'Can I speak to you privately?' Too late she realized the request was a glaring pointer to her guilt. For one fleeting moment she surprised an expression in his eyes that made her want to cry out to him, protesting her innocence.

For there was no doubt at all in her mind that in spite of all Olga had said Lean still hoped that Melanie could prove her innocence. And that could mean only one thing . . . that Lean cared. . . . Or had begun to care. . . . 'No, Melanie,' he said in soft and even tones. 'We shall go up to your room.'

Sick with helplessness and despair, she found speech difficult. What should she do? With bitter resignation she faced the fact that there was only one thing she could do.

'I have some money in my room,' she whispered huskily.

'How much?' Lean's face became set and hard, and the cold metallic glint returned to his eyes.

'Twenty-four pounds.'

Lean's eyes flickered; he said sharply,

'It's in English notes?'

Hope in his voice? No doubt of that, and Melanie's heart sank.

'It's in drachmae.' Glancing up, and meeting the exultant gaze of the girl who had proved far too clever for her, Melanie felt utterly defeated and drained. She could, of course, say where she had obtained the money, but she had given Kostagis her solemn promise and she could not go back on that. According to Giles, he would be liable to prosecution for illegally employing her. A sudden frown came to her brow. She *had* a work permit – Lean had obtained one for her, so why could she not work for Kostagis as well as Lean? But Giles must know what he was talking about, and his warning had been emphatic, impressing on Melanie the need for secrecy regarding her part-time work with the Greek couple. 'Do you admit taking the money?' Lean's voice was harsh and cold; he added without waiting for an answer to his question, 'You'd steal from my mother, who has befriended you?' He shook his head as if unable to comprehend such perfidy. 'Fetch the money down at once.' Such unspeakable disgust in his glance, such contempt in his tones. Melanie's lips trembled uncontrollably.

'I haven't stolen it,' she cried desperately. 'I swear it! You must believe me – you did over the earrings . . .'

'I did then, but not now.'

A little intake of Olga's breath diverted Melanie for a second. Her face was a study of exultation.

'Not . . .? You think I stole them, after all?'

Impatiently he sighed, and requested her once again to fetch the money down from her room.

'I shall be in my office,' he added, white lines of fury standing out from under the darkness of his skin. 'Bring it to me there and it will be returned to my mother.'

'It isn't your mother's money.' Melanie just had to say it.

His dark eyes swept over her again, then narrowed warningly.

'I don't expect any argument. Bring the money to my office immediately.'

Melanie hesitated. There seemed to be nothing for it but to do his bidding. It went very much against the grain to give up her money, and thereby admit to being a thief, but that was the simplest way. Trouble in plenty she would encounter if she persisted in protesting her innocence.

She brought down the money and was just about to enter the office when she stopped, deliberately listening to what was being said.

'I didn't say anything, because I realized you and she had once been friends, but she's a petty thief, Lean. I myself have missed money and several of the guests too—'

'The guests? There have been complaints? Who are they?'

Was he remembering that she had been able to pay the taxi driver five pounds? Melanie wondered, quivering with fury at what she heard.

'They've left now, but I did have complaints, Lean. I had an idea it was Melanie, but I couldn't be sure.'

Melanie entered, put the money on the desk, and walked out.

In view of what had happened Melanie felt disinclined to take over the new apartment and as some explanation to Sandra was necessary she told her exactly what had occurred.

Speechless for a moment, Sandra then exploded, threatening to go along to Olga's office to tell her exactly what she thought of her. Loyalty such as this was like balm to Melanie's wound, but she would not hear of Sandra's risking dismissal.

'I don't care,' Sandra declared hotly. 'Who wants to work in a place like this anyway?'

'While you're here life for me is at least bearable.'

'To think that hateful creature has your hard-earned money!'

'It wasn't exactly hard-earned.' Melanie gave a shrug. 'The loss of the money is the least of my worries,' she added, and Sandra said nothing, merely glancing perceptively at her.

Olga kept out of her way, but Richard was arriving on the Friday and Melanie went to the reception desk to see if accommodation were available.

'You want to reserve a single room for this friend?' Olga's lack of surprise revealed the fact of her having read Richard's letter, and an expression of disgust mingled with the cold contempt in Melanie's eyes. 'We have one only, and it's expensive. We have a suite, of course,' added Olga with a half-sneer.

'That will do.'

The older girl's eyes opened wide.

'Do you know the cost of it?'

'Will you book the suite for my friend? He'll be arriving after about six o'clock in the evening.'

Melanie had not been looking forward to Richard's visit; for one thing, she felt they now had nothing in common, and for another she rather dreaded the questions he would be sure to ask. But after her recent humiliating experience she found herself eagerly awaiting his arrival. He reached the hotel half an hour after Melanie had finished work; Kyrios came to her room, saying Richard had asked for her and she went immediately to his luxurious suite on the ground floor. For the first time since coming to Crete Melanie had taken particular care with her appearance; she had brought out one or two of the expensive models Richard had designed especially for her and she wore one of these. It was in a sort of rose-peach which gave an added beauty to her eyes and toned enchantingly with the delicate colour of her skin.

She had to pass the door leading to Lean's private rooms and just as she reached it Lean came striding out. They collided and instinctively Melanie clutched at his sleeve. He on the other hand took hold of her arm to steady her. For a fleeting moment they remained like that, with Melanie staring up at him, looking particularly adorable, and Lean gazing down at her as if he couldn't believe his eyes.

'I'm sorry.' Flushing, Melanie twisted away and hurried on towards the corridor off which were Richard's apartments. The flush still tinted her cheeks as she entered and Richard caught his breath in admiration.

'Melanie . . . you look lovelier than ever!'

And he seemed even more handsome than ever, she thought, moving aside as he would have taken her in his arms.

'It's good to see you, Richard,' she said, and meant it.

'You know why I've come?' He looked hurt by her action and Melanie felt faintly distressed. It would be as well, she decided, to make the position clear at once.

'I shall never marry,' she told him quietly. 'I can't say why, so please don't ask me.'

His grey eyes shadowed as they looked into hers.

'There's no need to ask, apparently. What's wrong? Is he married already?'

She shook her head, and moved over to the couch.

'Let's change the subject, Richard. Tell me everything about home and work. Is business as brisk as ever?'

'Business is as brisk as ever, and home is just the same

as it always was. Now, tell me your news?'

She smiled, in spite of herself, but hesitated a long while before speaking, and even then she was evasive, asking what he wanted to know. Everything, he told her, and again she hesitated.

'I suppose it's only fair, after you've travelled out to Crete, to tell you why I had to come here in the first place.' She sat down; Richard had already had drinks sent up and he began pouring her a sherry. 'I didn't tell you much before I left—'

'You didn't tell me anything – just handed in your notice, as if you were no more than an ordinary employee, and left me flat. I could get nothing out of you except apologies.'

'I was forced to come here, Richard, and work as a room maid, in order to pay off a debt.'

'*A room maid!*' His glass was half way to his mouth, and it remained there as he gaped at her. 'You said in your letters that you were employed here, but you never mentioned in what capacity.' His glance swept over her lovely figure, slim and elegant in the exquisitely-cut gown that had been especially fashioned for it. 'You're not serious?'

She smiled wanly and sipped her drink.

'This is the first time I've dressed up since coming here,' she confessed. 'I'm usually in severe black, with a white apron.'

He sat down opposite to her, a dark and uncomprehending frown creasing his brow. Melanie related, briefly, what had happened, omitting her humiliating experiences of being branded a thief, and as she noted his changing expression she began to wonder if she were doing right. For Richard was no coward, and he was now most certainly angry. If he should take it into his head to approach Lean then nothing Melanie could do would deter him.

'You've never mentioned this engagement,' he commented when at last she fell silent. 'You didn't love him, obviously . . . but now? Is he the man?'

Her lashes fluttered.

'Yes, Lean is the man.'

'And he doesn't return your love? What a damnable mess! But you can't stick in this place for another two years – a room maid! I won't have it, not with your talent! You're coming back to England with me.'

'No, I must clear off the debt.'

'I'll give you the money to pay off the debt. I'd have done so at first; you need only have asked me.'

'I've said the debt must be cleared in the way Lean stipulated. I agreed to this and there's nothing to be done.'

'Rubbish! The debt isn't yours for a start— What a vindictive man. You'd waste your thoughts on someone like that?'

She made no comment. It would be too difficult to convince Richard that Lean's hurt had gone very deep, that this revenge was conceived by the hatred that is akin to love.

'The money was merely a tool.' She murmured her thoughts aloud, bringing an angry exclamation from Richard.

'A debt's a debt, and can be settled by cash. I'll arrange for the money to be transferred—'

'I can't. . . .' She tailed off, allowing herself for one moment to dwell on the idea of freedom, of putting herself beyond the reach of Olga's vindictiveness and hate. But presently she shook her head. 'I can't borrow money from you.'

'I'm not offering to lend it.'

'But I couldn't accept it as a gift.'

He gazed into his glass, and her glance flickered over him to take in the clear-cut lines of his face, the artist's hands, and the immaculate suit he wore. She gave a little sigh. How simple everything would be if only she could care.

'Melanie, I meant what I said in my letter. I need you in the business, and I want to marry you – yes, there's this other man, but he's not for you. Come home, Melanie, take up your job again and we'll get right back where we were.'

Back . . . could one ever go back?

'I didn't know I cared, then, Richard.'

'You've learned to care only since coming here, it seems?'

'Yes, only since coming here.'

'Well, for the life of me I don't see why, not the way he's treated you.' He refilled her glass and then his own. 'You'll forget him. You're sensible, practical; this won't trouble you a jot six months from now.'

Could Richard be right? Would the memory of Lean fade as it had faded once before?

'I agreed to Lean's terms,' she persisted. 'I must pay the debt his way.'

'By sweat and tears? Oh, no, Melanie. Had I known what was going on I'd have been here sooner. He can't refuse a cash settlement. In any case, he's lucky that you're willing to pay at all.'

Melanie twisted the stem of the glass between her fingers, watching the changing colour as a shaft of sunlight added fire to the wine. Was the promise still binding – after the way he had been maligned? Another thought suddenly occurred to her. Perhaps Lean would welcome her departure, believing as he did that she could not be trusted to leave his guests' property alone.

'Richard,' she said impulsively, 'if you would lend me the money – I could come back and work for you and repay you out of my salary.' His brows lifted in surprise and Melanie added, 'I've had second thoughts; he might be glad to take the cash.'

'What's suddenly made you change your mind?'

'I can't tell you, Richard. But will you lend me the money?'

He hesitated.

'If you won't take it as a gift, then yes. But you'll come home?'

'Yes.'

'With me – when I go back in two weeks' time?'

She swallowed. Somehow, she knew she had come very close to happiness, to regaining the love of the man she had so thoughtlessly jilted, but Olga had triumphed and Melanie felt she must leave the island just as quickly as she could.

'If Lean will take the money – yes, I'll come home with you.' A wan smile touched her lips as she met his rather anxious gaze. 'I'll have to borrow my fare from you, as well.'

'We'll forget that, if you don't mind.'

They talked for a while, Richard making plans and telling her he would take her into partnership immediately.

'I should have done it before.' He shook his head regretfully. 'Tell me, honestly, would you have married me had I asked you a few months ago?'

'No, Richard,' she answered. 'I know now that I wouldn't.'

'Now? I said if I'd asked you a few months ago?'

She shook her head. 'No, I don't think I would.'

'You're not sure?'

She examined his face; he was merely curious as to her reply and she knew that her chief attraction for him was as an asset in his business. Nevertheless, he had wanted to marry her, and even now that she had refused him he was still willing to take her into partnership. She felt a deep sense of gratitude towards him. He trusted her implicitly and she did wonder what he would say were he to know how she had been treated by Olga and Lean. She would never tell him, or anyone else. When she left here in two weeks' time she would pick up the threads of her old life, throw herself into her work and endeavour to forget this hurtful and humiliating experience.

Richard suggested that Melanie inform Lean at once of the decision she had taken, pack her things and go with him to another hotel.

'We'll have a wonderful holiday – I'm sure you need it – and then fly home.'

But Melanie would not agree to this.

'Lean's terribly short staffed, and it's the busiest time of the year. I'll give him a fortnight's notice.'

'And continue working – while I'm here?' he frowned.

'I finish every day at four, and I have two days off a week. We'll get about, Richard. You can swim in the mornings, and do a bit of sightseeing afterwards; then we can go off somewhere each day just as soon as I've finished.' He did not like that idea, but Melanie smiled at him and the frown cleared instantly from his forehead.

'We'll begin right now,' he suggested, glancing at the clock. 'Afternoon tea on the lawn, followed by a shower and change of clothes, and off we go to find the most exclusive place in which to dine!'

She shook her head.

'We can't have tea on the lawn – at least, I can't, being one of the staff; and as I've no cocktail dress the dinner's out too – at the most exclusive place, at least. We can go to a less formal place where dress doesn't matter. . . .' Her voice trailed away into silence as she became aware of his changed expression.

'No dress? Now can you imagine my coming out here without bringing you a present?'

'A dress!' Unhappy as she was deep down inside, this gesture of Richard's made her eyes glow. 'An evening dress?'

He rose and went into the bedroom. Evidently he had already unpacked the dress, because he reappeared almost at once with the billowing creation over his arm.

'Now—' He wagged a finger at her and his eyes roved her figure in a clinical examination. 'If you've neither put on nor taken off an inch anywhere this should fit to perfection. We have your model still, so we fitted the dress to that.'

'Richard. . . .' Time seemed to drop away and she and Richard were once again working together. 'The line . . . the flounce. . . .' Automatically she held it to her and moved her body so that the skirt swung right out. 'You've used pure silk!'

'Silk and the net, of course. Like it?'

'It's lovely. The colour – it's a sort of mauve-cum-lilac, with the deep purple overskirt of net – oh, Richard, it's really superb!'

'Go and try it on – in the bedroom.'

Melanie went, thinking nothing of it. In their business one was always trying dresses on.

'I can't wear it, though,' she uttered in tones suddenly gone flat. 'I haven't any shoes.'

'Melanie dear . . .' he looked quizzically at her, 'do we ever forget the accessories?'

'You've brought shoes?'

'And wrap, and gloves and evening bag.'

She laughed, and for a little while her heart was light.

'Cinderella's going to the ball,' she said, and disappeared through the door of Richard's bedroom.

'Throw me that one you have on,' he requested after a moment or two. 'These French darts do something awfully good for the figure – not that *you* need to be slimmed, but I think we'll use them again in the spring models— Thanks,' he laughed as the dress came through the door. 'Yes ... we used these to very good effect last year. ...'

Melanie had slipped into the cocktail dress when she realized Richard had stopped speaking.

'Is someone there?' Cautiously she peered round the door. Richard was alone.

'No, someone went past – along the verandah. And did he stare! Looked at the dress in my hand as if he'd seen a ghost or something.'

Melanie's eyes moved to the window, taking up almost the whole of one wall. Normally that one was closed, for the verandah outside ran practically the length of the hotel and was in fact a public way. The other window opened on to an enclosed verandah which was, therefore, private. But Richard had flung wide the other window and anyone walking along the verandah would have a full view of the room inside.

'Who was it?'

Richard shrugged.

'I wouldn't know. Tall and dark and slim. A Greek, certainly.' He stared at her then whistled softly as she came across the room towards him. But Melanie's eyes were on the dress in Richard's hand. Was it Lean who had passed the window?

CHAPTER TEN

THEY had afternoon tea at another hotel and immediately on their return Melanie went along to Lean's office to inform him that she was leaving his employ. Her knock bringing no response, she tried his private apartment.

'Come in.' He evinced some surprise on seeing who it was, but as his expression changed she had no doubt at all that it was he who had passed the window and seen Richard with her dress in his hands. For Lean's glance swept insultingly over her, producing the sensation that she was being stripped. Flushing, she came straight to the point, telling him she would be leaving his service in a fortnight's time.

'As soon as I get to England I'll arrange for the thousand pounds to be returned to you,' she went on, her eyes suddenly clouding with regret. A leaden weight settled near her heart as she reflected on what might have been had not Olga by her lies and treachery succeeded in bringing her into disgrace for the second time. For the change in Lean's manner towards her had become so marked that Melanie had begun to cherish the hope that he would one day forgive her and happiness would be theirs. 'You can't refuse to accept the money,' she added, more concerned by the inflexible line of his jaw than by the puzzlement in his eyes.

'You have a thousand pounds?' he asked, watching her curiously.

'I can get it.'

A little silence and then,

'The arrangement was for you to work to pay off the debt.'

'You can't want me to stay,' she returned, faintly surprised that he had not accepted her offer with the minimum of comment. 'Not after what's happened. If I'm not to be trusted with the guests' property then it's better for you that I leave your employment.' Melanie did not stop to think that the unblushing manner in which she referred to her own apparent dishonesty might strike him as shameless, increasing the contempt and disgust he already felt for her.

'And you can find a thousand pounds, you say? – as simply as all that?'

She nodded and glanced away, wondering what he were thinking.

'I'm . . . borrowing it.'

Silence, and at length she turned her head. His lips were curved in a sneer.

'You're fortunate indeed, having a friend who is willing to loan you so large an amount of money.' The unveiled insinuation brought the colour rushing to her cheeks; she knew he was seeing Richard holding her dress and suddenly she could take no more. Her eyes blazed and fury blanked out everything except the desire to hit back.

'I'm borrowing it from the man I'm going to marry!'

'Marry?' For a brief moment he seemed to be lost for words. 'You were engaged before you came out here?' The contempt had gone from his glance and tone; he appeared to be under some slight strain as he waited, tensed, for her answer to his question.

She swallowed, already regretting that impulsive lie. Reluctant to lie again, yet unable to retract, she merely expressed her unwillingness to discuss her private affairs with him. He stiffened at the curtness of her tones; became thoughtful for a while and then shrugged indifferently.

'You'll be leaving in two weeks' time, you say?' And then he added, as the thought occurred to him, 'Why not now?'

'You're short-staffed; I felt it would give you time to find a replacement for me.'

Lean's eyes flickered strangely. This, and an almost imperceptible shake of his head, portrayed his perplexity at her consideration, but as no comment appeared to be forthcoming Melanie accepted his silence as a dismissal and left him without another word.

Sandra came into her room just as she was ready to go out to dinner with Richard. A low whistle left her lips as Melanie turned, her wrap over her arm, and smiled at her.

'My, but you look absolutely stunning!'

'Thank you.' Melanie flushed, and her smile deepened. But her eyes were clouded, for all the time she was dressing, taking such care with her appearance, her thoughts were with Lean. If only it were he who was taking her out to dinner. She picked up her evening bag and wrap. 'I feel like Cinderella,' she laughed, although a little shakily. 'It's such a long time since I dressed up.'

'Did you always have beautiful clothes like this?' Sandra glanced a trifle enviously at her. 'I suppose Richard always designed them for you?'

'Latterly, yes. Not when I first went to work for him, because at that time I was no different from the other girls in his employ.'

'But then you became his favourite?'

She nodded.

'I was lucky; several titled women liked my designs, so Richard began to – well, to notice me.'

'Will you marry him, do you think?' There was a hint of regret in her voice and Melanie instinctively sensed that she was thinking of Lean.

'No, Sandra,' she returned, slipping a dainty lace handkerchief into her bag. 'I shall never marry anyone.'

'Never?' Sandra shook her head. 'One can't say a thing like that. The future is always unpredictable.'

'True; but marriage is not for me.'

'You're in love with the boss, aren't you?'

'Yes,' she replied after a tense little silence. 'And that's why I shall never marry.'

Richard said he would wait for her in the foyer, and she had originally meant to use the servants' staircase and go round to the front of the hotel from the outside. But for some reason which she felt was quite out of character she had an urge to use the main stairway. Perhaps it was that she no longer considered herself an employee . . . certainly she did not feel like the despised little room maid who was for ever enduring the criticism and complaints of Olga Newson.

There was a small bar at one side of the foyer and as Melanie reached the top of the stairs she saw that in addition to the several guests who were standing at the bar, Lean and his mother and Eleni were seated close by, their drinks on the table in front of them. All heads were turned as Melanie came downstairs, her lovely dress a model of perfection, setting off the graceful tender curves of her body. The attention and interest made little impression upon her; certainly it did not disconcert her. For in her job at home she had often modelled the dresses which both she and Richard designed, so she descended the wide staircase with the old assurance of manner, assuming that air of distinction and proud indifference without which a model would never reach the pinnacle of success.

Her glance flickered to Lean, held his for a second before passing fleetingly to his mother and finally to his sister. And then she looked straight at Olga, sitting there at the reception desk. The older girl opened her eyes wide as if unable to take in what she saw. Melanie could almost hear the little inward gasp as, literally floating past her, she gave Richard the smile his clients had come to know so well.

He took her arm and together they left the hotel; the taxi was waiting and Richard handed her in. 'You look like a queen,' he said when they were seated in the cab. 'I've surpassed myself with that dress.'

Melanie had to smile. No compliment, his remark about her looking like a queen. He ought not to marry, she decided, for he had nothing to offer a wife, dedicated as he was to his work. He lived with it, and Melanie recalled that even when he did take her out in the old days his glance had been roving round, examining with a businesslike eye every dress that happened to be attractive enough to claim his attention.

They chose the Astir, and immediately they entered the hotel every eye was turned in Melanie's direction. Again she accepted the admiring glances without a trace of embarrassment. But she was interested, for in her modesty she saw those glances directed only at the beautiful gown she wore.

'You're going to be famous soon,' she remarked as they sat down at the table.

'I'm already famous,' he returned, smiling at her and at the same time picking up the wine list.

'I should have said *very* famous.'

'*We* are to be very famous. It's a partnership from now on, remember.'

A partnership. ... How thrilled she would have been had he offered that a few months ago – before the renewal of her acquaintanceship with Lean. To be so highly rewarded for her work was a circumstance that had never entered into her ambitions. On becoming Richard's chief assistant she had believed herself to have reached the point from which she could proceed no higher. And now she was to be a partner. She gave a quivering sigh of regret; it was ironical that she should be denied the elation which would normally have been consequent on the acquiring of such a coveted position, for she felt certain that Richard's would one day be the most important fashion house in London.

Although it was very late when they returned to the Hotel Avra Lean's light was still on. Later, unable to sleep, Melanie left her bed and, standing on the chair, looked through the opening that served as a window. It was a clear night with millions of stars twinkling from a purple sky and a crescent moon hanging over the sea. She stayed there a long while, fully aware of the reason for her restlessness and wondering just how long it would be before tranquillity of mind was restored to her. Once back home, with all her time and energy devoted to her work, she might be able to forget Lean ... forget ...? Instinctively her eyes flickered to the garden below Reflected light on the grass in front of Lean's bedroom window told her that he, too, was unable to sleep.

Lean's mother and sister had left the hotel – Madam Angeli to return to her home near Athens and Eleni to return to London. An English girl, Pauline, had come to work for Lean and she had the little apartment which Melanie and Sandra had so laboriously cleaned and scrubbed. Pauline was engaged to a Cretan boy whom she had met in England. He was finishing his education there and Pauline had decided to come to Crete for a few months in order to discover whether or not she could settle here. From the first she extended friendliness to both girls and Melanie felt glad for Sandra's sake that Pauline had come to work at the hotel.

'I shall miss you just the same,' Sandra declared one evening when Melanie was sitting with her in her room. Melanie had been to see Androula and Kostagis, giving them their final lesson and bidding them goodbye. On informing Richard of her intention, he had raised objections, but Melanie could not bring herself to do as he suggested and merely telephone them. And so Richard had reluctantly agreed to go off on his own for one evening. The Greek couple had expressed regret that she was leaving the island, and so profuse had been their goodbyes that they had completely forgotten about her fee. Not that this last couple of pounds mattered, she thought, recollecting with intense bitterness that not only had all her earnings from this source gone into Olga Newson's pocket, but it was Melanie's possession of the money that had made possible the success of Olga's plan to brand her a thief for the second time. 'We must write to one another,' Sandra was saying. 'And when I finally do settle down we can renew our friendship.'

Melanie agreed, although she did go on to ask when Sandra thought she would have had enough of this travelling and be able to settle down in a routine job in England. Sandra grinned, began to say that it might not be too long, and then stopped.

'I love this island, though – it sort of grows on you, and if I could get a decent job, a more refined job, I think I'd stay. This present one's all right in that it serves its purpose, but I couldn't do it indefinitely.'

'I agree. It isn't at all suitable. What sort of work would you like?'

'Frankly, I'd be in my element with Olga's position. And I think I could do it—' She shrugged, then added, 'Olga's a permanent fixture, though. Not that the boss likes her still. I'm very sure he doesn't, but I have to admit she's efficient, and that's what's important to the boss.'

'Perhaps you could get that sort of post elsewhere.'

'To be honest, I've tried. But when they ask me what I'm doing now it's hardly any recommendation to say I'm a room maid.'

'But they can tell you're capable of doing something much better.' Melanie's eyes flashed indignantly. 'They could at least give you a trial; they'd soon discover your capabilities then!'

'Thanks.' Sandra laughed but shook her head. 'There are people with experience and naturally they land the jobs. No, it'll have to be England eventually, unless I find I still like my Arab, and decide to marry him.'

'I don't think you'd marry an Arab,' laughed Melanie, and after only the merest hesitation Sandra nodded her head in agreement.

'No . . . they're too Eastern.'

Lean was Eastern, but his culture and command of English, the equality with which he treated his sister and his enlightened attitude towards her – all these were so different from what Melanie had learned of the average Greek and his adherence to the old traditions. It was only if she should happen to recall Lean's reaction to the broken engagement that she would remember he was all Greek, that his ancestors were pagans, ruthless and cruel. The long years of nursing a grievance and the unhesitating way in which he had seized the opportunity of revenge . . . these reflected the primitive instincts hidden beneath an exterior of refinement and polish. Perhaps, she mused as if half seeking consolation for what she had lost, life would have been most unpleasant had she married a man so vastly different from herself. He would be master, that was for sure, and while she owned to herself that at seventeen she had found his mastery exciting, she was not at all sure she would be so thrilled by it now.

However, these conjectures were a waste of time, for everything between Lean and herself was over – or would be in four days' time when she left the island to return with Richard to England.

A new life and a new position. .... She must forget Lean, she decided, while at the same time freely admitting that the renewal of the acquaintanceship with her ex-fiancé had left a wound so deep that much time would pass before its scar was erased.

The following day, Wednesday, she and Richard set out early in the car he had hired complete with driver. They stopped in town for a short while, wandering round the Venetian harbour. Everything had an air of romance about it – the golden weathered bastions, the colourful caiques, twin-masted and lying placidly in a sea of vividly contrasting colours. In a lambent sky the sun climbed steadily, promising a scorching day.

'What are they doing that for?' Melanie shuddered on seeing a small group of youths slapping a newly-caught octopus against the rocks. 'It's not dead.'

'Of course it's not dead,' he laughed. 'This is their way of killing it. I should have thought you'd have seen them doing this before. You don't appear to have seen anything since coming here.'

There had been so little time, she reflected, feeling regretful at the idea of leaving the island without having explored its beauties a little more.

'Let's go,' she said, loath to stay and witness this cruelty, but Richard shook his head. He wanted to see it die, which it eventually did, slowly and painfully. An all-enveloping feeling of depression swept over Melanie. What was wrong that one thing had to kill another in order to survive? And what was wrong with people like Richard, who could derive pleasure – or

was it merely satisfaction? – from watching such bar-
barism as this. For the boys had begun to scrub it; this
scrubbing produced a foam rather like soap-suds
which, when the octopus was rinsed, left it beautifully
clean.

They moved at last; above them houses jostled
together, sun-bleached doors and shutters peeling;
palms swaying, scented pines, and soft hills rising,
rugged mountains capped with snow. Beyond the Venetian harbour the modern quay gave access to the
gaily-festooned white cruise ships, bringing their voy-
agers to spend enough time on the island to visit the
magnificent Palace of Minos before sailing away to take
a fleeting glimpse of another Greek island.

'We must come here again, for a proper holiday,'
Richard said with decision. 'I like this island very much
indeed.' His glance swept the enchanting scene and he
became thoughtful. Cutting the line between the sea
and sky were the hills of Dragon, the barren island on
which Hera in her wrath confined the beautiful
nymph, Dia, born as a result of one of Zeus's incredibly
numerous amours.

'This background. ...' He stopped, spreading his
hands in an all-embracing movement. 'Can't you imagine our models standing about ... here? One or two
sitting on that rock ... ?' He tailed off as Melanie
laughed.

'Don't you ever think of anything else but work?'

'I'm an artist,' he protested, flashing her an indig-
nant glance. 'I see pictures everywhere. This old harbour would make a magnificent backcloth for certain
of my new models.'

Melanie said nothing and they wandered into the
town. After refreshments of kebabs on little sticks and
minute cups of thick sweet coffee they drove to Kritsa.
It was a fascinating 'film-set' village of flowers and

trees and wide terraces looking out over the olive and carob valley to the sea and the Gulf of Mirabello. Their destination was Leto and soon they were in the car again, continuing on their way. But the road became so stony and narrow that they left the car and after scrambling over rocks and along a narrow goat track they finally reached the spread of ruins that marked the site of the ancient city-state of Archaic-Hellenic days.

'The view!' gasped Melanie when, as they stood on a sort of ledge between the heights, she gazed with faint awe on to the crags and sheer rock faces which culminated in sharp and rugged peaks. In the other direction was a great valley with precipitous sides, laden with gnarled and twisted olives, with here and there the brighter, shining foliage of the carob trees, contrasting with the vast flutter of silver-grey as the leaves of the ancient olives trembled in the breeze.

As so often happens in Greece, a villager appeared, from out of nowhere it seemed. From his brown and wizened face a pair of piercing, intelligent eyes regarded them as the man asked in excellent English,

'You want to look around? I shall help you if you wish?'

'What luck,' commented Richard a few minutes later, for their self-appointed guide knew all the history of the ancient site.

'It was a Hellenic town in the seventh century B.C.,' the guide said over his shoulder as he led the way to the *agora*. 'But these ruins date mainly from the third century B.C. At that time Leto was a very important city-state and its port was Ayios Nikolaos, which you can see down there below. So if their port was attacked they would be warned; this gives you a good idea of how clever they were in choosing sites for their settlements.' They lingered in the *agora*, and Melanie tried to visualize this market place when it was bustling with life. On the altar of Hestia a lamp had burned perpetually, their guide told them as they moved on to explore the ruined houses and shops, the cisterns and the temple.

'This was the magistrate's house, and here they had all the civic buildings.' Flowers and weeds grew over the broken columns, but as with most of these historical sites nothing could take away the impression of grandeur, or cloud the imagination of anyone willing to see the splendour of those days when the savage, yet noble athlete would depart from the island to compete in the Olympic Games. Should he be a winner he would on his return be fêted by the whole community and crowned with the coveted olive wreath.

On the way home they stopped at Mallia for tea, and as Richard had not previously been there they wandered around for a while before finally returning to the car and making for Heraklion. There was just time for a hurried shower and change before they were off, once more to dine at the Astir.

Although Melanie was awake early the following morning she lay there, staring unseeingly at the flaking plaster and deep cracks above her head. Two more days. . . . Tomorrow night she was finishing here, and early Saturday morning she and Richard would be on their way to the airport. Melanie had already written to her parents; they at least would welcome her release from the contract she had verbally made with Lean. A tinge of guilt suddenly affected her and she frowned. True, she had broken her word, but after the way in which she had been treated she felt herself absolved from that promise. Not that it was Lean's fault, for to him her guilt must seem to have been conclusively proved, especially after her apparent dishonesty back in England. Nevertheless, she had known unbearable hurt when, after saying he believed her over the question of Mrs. Skonson's earrings, he had gone back on his word. Yes, he deserved that she should break her promise, and Melanie could find no reason at all for these irritating qualms of conscience that refused to be shaken off.

Richard had gone off on an organized trip to Knossos. This was in response to Melanie's persuasion, for it was unthinkable that he should visit Crete without seeing this magnificent centre of early Minoan civilization. Richard would not return until seven o'clock, when he and Melanie would go out to dine and dance. Meanwhile, having finished her work at four, Melanie felt at a loose end, as Sandra was out too, having gone off to visit some friends living at Poros, just outside Heraklion. Deciding to go on to Sandra's balcony and read, Melanie made herself some sandwiches and tea in the little kitchen and took the tray out to the shady corner over which grew the vines. A fresh breeze came from the sea, stirring the palm fronds and tossing the flower heads so that their perfume mingled with that of the pines. She sat back, her tea on the table in front of her, a sandwich on the plate on her knee. Voices registered vaguely, for her thoughts were confused. Her one desire was to leave here, yet every moment was becoming precious. Every glimpse of Lean, every snatch of his voice in some other room or part of the grounds. . . .

Every snatch of his voice—

'No, I'm afraid she isn't. A friend of hers is over from England and she's been going off every afternoon immediately on finishing work.'

Frowning, Melanie leaned forward, straining to peer through the railings, but she saw nothing. Lean and his companion must be on the verandah outside the lounge. Who could be asking for her? She heard

Lean's voice as he offered refreshment, heard the waiter's respectful reply, and then the indistinct conversation between Lean and his visitor. Should she go down? But what could she do? She could scarcely enter the garden and approach Lean, nor could she go through the lounge, for the staff were not allowed in there either.

It was about ten minutes later that she realized who it was, and she knitted her brows. What could Kostagis want with her?

He was going and Melanie could hear his voice plainly as, standing up, he moved from the shade of the verandah into the open. Both he and Lean were immediately under the balcony where she sat, and although on first hearing Kostagis's voice she had risen, with the intention of going down, she changed her mind, her curiosity getting the better of her.

'I'm still sure I know you by sight. I've seen you somewhere.'

'As I've already said, I'm quite sure you're mistaken.' Lean's voice was polite enough, but to Melanie's ears at least it held a hint of impatience.

'Perhaps you're right, and yet – I have it! You've just bought a house at Khania, on a hill overlooking the sea. It has the most magnificent view I've ever seen!'

'What makes you think I've just bought it?' Something very odd in Lean's tones and Melanie waited curiously for Kostagis's reply.

'It's been empty for about six or seven years – terribly neglected. My wife and I have friends nearby and they tell us it had new owner at last and that it was being renovated. Naturally we have a good look the next time we passed. You were in the garden with the contractor, I assume?' No answer, and Kostagis went on, 'My friends say the man who buy the house was a

176

hotel owner. I expect you're tired of living with your business, yes?'

'I did think it would be a change to live in a house,' agreed Lean with more friendliness than Melanie would have expected.

'Well, I hope you have better luck with it than the two previous owners.'

'Two?' repeated Lean sharply.

'You don't know its history? The man who build it was an English millionaire, but he die just before it was finished. Then a wealthy young Greek buy it and immediately engaged an army of workmen to put the finishing touches to it. He intended bringing his English bride there, so the rumour goes, but the marriage never take place.' He paused; Melanie felt the use go out of her legs and she sank into the chair, her whole body trembling as she waited to hear more. 'So upset, he was, this young man, that he never went near it again. But you've got it in time – it's only the paint-work that's gone, and the grounds, of course. Somewhere under those weeds and other rubbish is a wonderful swimming-pool, I believe?'

'That's correct; there is.'

'You'll soon get it into shape again – and I hope you'll be happy there. Third time lucky, so they say,' he added with a laugh.

Melanie watched him go, saw him turn and give a salutatory wave of the hand to Lean, who stood under her balcony. But Lean was apparently staring into space, for he made no response to Kostagis's friendly gesture.

For a long while Melanie could not move; it seemed as if her body were completely weighed down by guilt. How could she have done that terrible thing to Lean . . . Lean who had loved her so deeply? No wonder he had grasped at the chance of revenge, no wonder he had wanted to see her suffer.

And now he was doing up the house. . . .

What did it mean? Melanie had often wondered if he were content to live at the hotel. As a bachelor it was perhaps all right, but even so she had not felt he was in his right environment. There was nothing solid or permanent in hotel life and she often felt that Lean was totally unsuited to it. His very strength gave the impression of stability, and there was no stability in a hotel existence.

Why had Kostagis come? she wondered, and then remembered that he had forgotten to pay her for that last lesson. He would not have left the money with Lean, on account of having to remain secretive about employing her, but he would most certainly have left a message. However, Melanie was quite unable to go down, after what she had just overheard, and she fervently hoped Lean would send the message with Kyrios in the morning. In this way there would merely be the goodbyes to be said, and those in Richard's presence if it were at all possible, for the last thing Melanie desired was to find herself alone with Lean, overwhelmed as she was by this remorse and regret.

She was still on the balcony when she saw Sandra coming along the road. Looking up, Sandra waved, but it was over a quarter of an hour later that she entered the room – bounded in would be a better description, Melanie thought, turning to scan her friend's flushed countenance.

'Melanie! You'll never guess!' Sandra came out on to the balcony, her eyes sparkling as she sat down on a deck chair opposite to Melanie. 'I'm the new receptionist!'

'You're—?' Melanie blinked at her. 'What do you mean?'

'Olga's gone!'

'Gone?' echoed Melanie in blank bewilderment. 'Gone where?'

'Sacked – out on her heels!'

Sacked? Was it possible that Lean had at last discovered the truth?

'She was there a couple of hours ago when I came off duty,' she began, when Sandra interrupted her.

'Listen while I tell you exactly what happened,' she said, and went on to say that immediately on entering the hotel fifteen minutes ago Sandra had been called into the office by Lean, who at once asked her if she would take over the desk as from the following morning. 'I asked if Olga were ill, and you should have seen his expression; he looked like thunder. She wasn't ill, he said, but she had left the hotel, so there was this vacancy. He said to try it for a week and if I like it – and he was suited with me – I could have the post permanently. Isn't it wonderful?' She waited expectantly, but for a moment Melanie was too dazed to congratulate her. If Olga was there two hours ago, then something must have happened since then. . . .

'How do you know she was sacked?'

'I saw Kyrios on my way up here just now and I asked him what had happened. I knew he'd be able to give me some information because he never misses anything. He said the boss had Olga in his office and was telling her off; the next moment she came out looking as white as a sheet and went upstairs to pack. Within an hour she had put her things in her car and gone off. It's obvious the boss has found her out at last.'

'Yes . . . but how?'

'Couldn't say, but he was bound to some time, wasn't he?'

'Perhaps . . . but she was always so clever.'

'Oh, I don't know. She wasn't very clever when she let Madam Angeli hear her talking to you like that.

The boss has been pretty cool towards her since then. I've heard him speaking abruptly to her on several occasions lately.'

But he had believed her over the stolen money, reflected Melanie, her mouth curving bitterly. If only he had found Olga out a little sooner. . . .

Melanie decided not to wait for the message to be sent to her and when she and Richard left the hotel later she asked Richard if she could call on Kostagis. As his house was not too far distant they reached it in a few minutes by taxi. Richard waited outside and Melanie ran up the steps and rang the bell.

'Melanie!' Androula opened wide the door and Melanie entered the hall. 'Kostagis came to see you, to pay monies he owe, but you not in. Did you see Mr. Angeli? He pay you the monies?'

Melanie's eyes opened wide.

'Kostagis paid the money to Mr. Angeli—?'

'Melanie. . . .' Kostagis came in, all smiles. 'You should have reminded me of money I owed. Mr. Angeli give it to you?'

'Kostagis,' she breathed, in some dismay, 'you know about the need for secrecy . . . I mean, we shouldn't have let anyone know I was working for you.' Even as she spoke the more momentous aspect of this was striking her forcibly. If Lean knew she had been earning money, then— She caught her breath. He had dismissed Olga only a short while after Kostagis's visit! 'You told Mr. Angeli I'd been working for you for some time?'

'Certainly. For there was no need for secrecy, after all.'

'No need?' she echoed quiveringly, and Kostagis shook his head.

'That's right. I have a friend who lawyer, and he tell me there is no problem, because already you have the work permit.'

'When did you know this, Kostagis? – that it was permissible to work for you, I mean?'

'Right away, because I think to myself that we shall all be in trouble if we are breaking the law. So I make – what you say? – discreet inquiries, and this friend he say it is all right. I mean to tell you, but I forget.' He shrugged. 'It is no matter.'

No matter. Melanie could have wept.

All the while she was keeping quiet, allowing Olga to brand her a thief, and even handing over that money, her caution had been unnecessary. Everything was clear now, though. On learning from Kostagis that she, Melanie, had been earning money Lean had sent for Olga and, it seemed reasonable to assume, had questioned her more closely about the affair of the theft from his mother's handbag. Olga must have broken down – and Melanie could easily imagine that too, if Lean had treated her to anything like the scene to which Melanie herself had once been treated on being foolish enough to arouse his wrath.

Lean was waiting for her when she and Richard arrived back at the hotel after dining at the Astir. He came from the bar where he had been sitting talking to one of the guests.

'Melanie,' he said, without even a glance at Richard, 'I would like to speak to you.' Such a quiet tone, and accents so different from those which were familiarly edged with contempt and disgust. 'In my sitting-room, please.'

'Yes.' Her heart fluttered. Was it not too late, after all? 'Will you excuse me, Richard?'

He looked far from pleased, and for a space Melanie thought he would make some demur. But eventually he shrugged, said good night, nodded to Lean, and then left them alone.

Lean did not speak as he led the way to the door leading to his suite. On entering the sitting-room he stepped aside and she preceded him. Closing the door, he stood for a moment with his back to it, regarding her in silence.

'May I take your wrap?' he asked at length, coming forward and extending a hand. She gave him the wrap and once more his eyes roved over her. She blushed and lowered her head. 'Sit down,' invited Lean, carefully draping her wrap over the back of one of the chairs. 'I have some money for you.'

'Yes.'

'You know?' He gazed down at her in surprise before, bringing up a chair, he seated himself on the opposite side of the wide marble fireplace.

'I was in when Kostagis called – upstairs on Sandra's balcony. Also I've been to see him. He said you had the money.' Her heart was beating far too quickly, and she had to clasp her hands together in order to stop the nervous twitching of her fingers. 'I called on him because I guessed why he had been here.'

Her words had an odd effect on Lean. His eyes narrowed and his voice became harshly accusing.

'You allowed me to believe Olga, to accuse you of theft, when all the time you had actually earned the money in your possession. I'd like your explanation, if you please.'

'I – thought I was breaking the law, thought I shouldn't be doing two jobs.' He looked at her in puzzlement and she went on to explain further. His black brows came together in a frown.

'You actually believed a thing like that? I should have given you credit for more sense. I had obtained a work permit for you and that was all that was required. Your friend must have been misinformed.'

'I realize that now.'

'And it was out of this money that you paid for the taxi.' He spoke to himself, the frown on his brow deepening. But after a while his face cleared and he looked a trifle tired, she thought. His changed expression did not take away the arrogance from his mouth, though, or alter that air of god-like superiority. 'I owe you an apology,' he said at last, and the manner of his speech betrayed the difficulty he underwent in owning to that. 'I'm sorry, Melanie, both for accusing you on that occasion, and also on the previous occasion. It's probably of little interest to you now, but Olga has gone from here; she's no longer in my employ.'

'I know. . . .' Her mouth felt dry, but she added, 'Sandra told me about her new post.' Dejection was slowly creeping over her as his words of a moment ago registered. 'It's probably of little interest to you now. . . .'

He did not want her, then.

'The money – that which was brought by your friend, Kostagis, and also that taken from your room by Olga – is there, on the table just behind you.'

She turned, but did not touch the roll of notes lying at her elbow.

'You managed to get it back from Olga?' She gave a tiny shrug. 'It didn't matter.'

'Most certainly it mattered.' His tone was edged with steel, and as Melanie noted the swift anger in his eyes a tingle shot along her spine. Olga had certainly lived through an unpleasant few minutes before receiving her dismissal. 'The money belongs to you.' He paused; Melanie felt tensed and half rose from her chair. But before she had time to carry out her intention of bidding him good night he spoke, asking if he could get her a drink. 'It's only half-past eleven,' he said, noting her eyes flicker to the clock on the wall.

She accepted the drink, even though she did not want it, and a moment or two later she was holding the glass to her lips.

'What time are you going on Saturday?' he inquired in casual tones.

'Early. Our plane leaves at ten.'

'Ten. . . .' His own eyes strayed absently to the clock. Melanie had the extraordinary impression that he was actually counting the hours!

'You're soon to be married, you said. How soon?'

Married? She had forgotten that. How stupid to lie. What could she tell him?

'I – well, I'm not – not—'

'Not waiting too long? Is that what you're trying to say? But why the blushes?' His glance flicked her mockingly. 'No, don't wait too long, Melanie, or you might change your mind!'

The colour left her face; quite unexpectedly she felt afraid of him.

'I must be going.' She spoke awkwardly. The air was electrified, but it was not that which affected Melanie and produced in her a desire to be gone. It was the tenseness in Lean himself. So calm and controlled on the surface . . . but Melanie experienced the terrifying sensation of being in the presence of some wild animal, sleek and sinewed and ready to pounce. She left her chair, and with a sort of strategic movement, made for the door. Lean spoke softly, his lips drawn back just sufficiently for her to see a row of even white teeth. His accents were guttural, coming from the back of the throat . . . like the low ominous growl that precedes the vicious attack.

'Don't go without your money,' he said, making no attempt to hand it to her. Melanie swallowed, endeavouring to release the tight little ball of fear that threatened to choke her.

'I – y-yes, my m-money. . . .' She would rather have left it there, for Lean had risen and was standing by the chair she had just vacated . . . and she would have to pass so very close to him.

Having picked up the notes Melanie turned, to find her way barred; she stepped to one side and Lean with a lightning movement snatched at her wrist.

'Leave go of me!' Her eyes dilated, for she knew this man, had once before encountered this unbridled savage, this dark pagan who, moved neither by her pleas nor her tears, had let her feel his strength, subjecting her to a violent onslaught that had left her quaking and bruised and wishing she had never had the misfortune to set eyes on him.

As she made a move to twist from his hold his grip tightened mercilessly and she abruptly ceased her struggles.

'So you're to be married, are you?' His voice snarled; his face assumed an expression of darkest evil. 'We'll see about that—!'

'Let me go!' Melanie began struggling again, but her puny efforts were stayed as Lean pressed her arms to her sides. His dark face came down, almost touching hers; she noted the smouldering embers of desire in his eyes, felt the possessiveness of his hold as he drew her close. His kiss left her weak and she would have fallen, she felt sure, had he released her. But he did not release her.

'You're to be married,' he repeated in the same snarling accents. '*Married!*' The word inflamed him and as Melanie, stunned, realized this, she hastened to rectify the lie she had so senselessly told him.

'Lean . . . when I said about marriage—' But she was cut short as he crushed her to him again, his mouth hard and ruthless as it possessed her lips and her throat and then moved to her shoulder where the tiny sleeve of her dress had slipped down, helped by Lean's rough handling of her.

'There'll be no wedding in England for you, my girl! You're to be married – yes! But to me, do you hear? It's marriage to me or immediate prosecution for your brother. I've no need to trouble myself as to the choice you'll make!'

Marriage.... To this primitive savage! He dropped his hands to his sides and she glanced first at one of her arms and then at the other, frowning at the vivid red marks he had left there.

'You agreed to accept the money.' She scarcely knew what she said, so chaotic were her thoughts.

'I've changed my mind. I should have insisted on marriage at the very beginning, but I despised you so. Even for the opportunity of inflicting a more severe punishment on you I didn't consider it was worth saddling myself with a thief for a wife. But you're not a thief; I know that now. Nevertheless, I'm using your brother's crime to get what I want – and that is you! For seven years I've wanted you – you're mine! Mine, do you hear?'

Melanie moved away and he made no attempt to stop her. She stared down fascinatedly at the notes, scattered on the rug by the fireplace. She hadn't the vaguest recollection of dropping them.

Marriage.... That he loved her she had not the slightest doubt, and that he had been renovating the house with marriage in mind she had no doubt either. Marriage to a man like this.... She looked at him, his face remained darkly evil, his nostrils were still flared.

'You're blackmailing me into marriage? You're really saying that unless I agree to be your wife you'll prosecute my brother?'

'Correct!'

She watched him intently. Despite that outward fury, he was clearly suffering. Perhaps he knew deep down inside that, should she insist on offering him the cash payment, he would in the end be forced to accept it.

She turned her back to him, putting a finger out to touch the exquisite little Roman tear bottle she had previously admired.

'If – if you l-loved me ... there would be no – no need for threats.' Her words came with difficulty, not only because of what they were meant to convey, but also because Melanie was so deeply affected both by the depth of her own emotions and the violence of the attack she had just endured.

A long silence followed her faltering admission of love and Lean approached her so softly that she was unaware of his nearness until she felt his hands upon her shoulders. Gently he turned her round to face him, but he had to tilt her chin himself before he could look into her eyes and seek there for what he so avidly desired to find.

'Melanie,' he whispered huskily at last, 'do you know what you've just said?' But he did not wait for an answer as, sweeping her into his arms, he kissed her – this time so very differently from before. 'I've loved you so long, my darling – from the moment I saw your face I desperately wanted you for my own.'

Tears sprang to her eyes, but she managed to blink them away.

'I was such a fool, but seventeen is a stupid age.' She shook her head regretfully. 'One doesn't know what life is all about, Lean. But I'm not making excuses, because I was old enough to realize that people could be hurt.' He drew her close to him again, seeming to be lost for words, and she murmured softly, 'Forgive me, Lean. I'll make it up to you. I promise.'

It was past midnight when he said, smiling tenderly at her as she sat beside him on the couch,

'I have a wonderful house for us, Melanie. It's on a hill, with magnificent views. I hope you'll like it. I'll take you to see it in the morning. It won't be ready for another fortnight, so we can't go into it immediately on our marriage—'

'Can't?' She had been on the verge of tears again as he talked about the house, knowing as she did that he had intended bringing her to it seven years ago, but his last words diverted her. 'When are we to be married?'

'Immediately!' The familiar set of his mouth and jaw, the light in his eyes that warned of the futility of argument. 'I've waited long enough. We shall be married just as soon as I can arrange it – which should be in two or three days at most.' He waited for her reaction. She agreed to be married at once, and went on to tell him, hesitantly, that she had overheard him and Kostagis talking about the house at Khania.

'I felt so dreadful,' she admitted contritely. 'But I was miserable, too, for I knew I loved you and thought there was no hope for me at all.'

'There would have been hope for ever,' he declared, his voice vibrant with emotion. But immediately he changed the subject. 'I left the house empty, as you heard, but when you'd been here a while I began to hope again that we'd marry—' Melanie had put a hand tenderly against his cheek and he brought it to his mouth and kissed it. 'I felt that you had now learned to love me a little, so I set to work on the house a second time—'

'I noticed the change in your manner towards me,' she cut in eagerly, 'and I too began to hope. For at that time you didn't believe I'd stolen those earrings and there seemed very little to stand in the way— But then

Olga did that awful thing and you started to hate me again.'

'Hate?' His arm tightened lovingly and the tenderness of his eyes took her breath away and made her wonder if the man she had seen half an hour ago was real. 'Melanie, when a Cretan loves it's for always. With all those misunderstandings I did come to despise you, I admit, but never for a moment have I ceased to love you.' He kissed her with infinite gentleness and then reverted to the topic of the house. 'I was going to ask you to come and see it, and propose to you there, in the garden, when it was quite ready, but then came the affair of Mother's money. I was shattered and once more work on the house came to a halt.' He looked apologetically at her. 'I really have no excuse for believing Olga, Melanie. Forgive me, dearest.'

'You had to believe her,' she argued generously. 'Everything pointed to my guilt – and – and especially after what had happened in England. No, you mustn't blame yourself, darling. We had Olga against us and we should be eternally thankful that the truth has come out before it's too late.'

'Were you really going to marry this fellow Melton?' he asked, frowning darkly, yet at the same time regarding her in extreme perplexity. 'You'd have married him, while loving me?'

She shook her head, blushing as she was forced to tell him why she had lied. It was because of the suspicious way he had looked and spoken, she added, staring apologetically at him.

'I suppose there was an excuse,' he conceded, and then, his voice suddenly edged with anger, 'I saw him with your dress in his hand— Yes, what the devil was he doing with that?'

'He's a dress designer. . . .' She tailed off, realizing how little Lean knew of her. She proceeded to give him a brief picture of what she had done with her life from the moment he had left her. 'It was quite natural for him to ask me to try the evening dress on,' she added on almost reaching the end of her story. But she did glance at him rather fearfully, for his mouth had suddenly tightened and his eyes had acquired an icy glint. 'He – he asked me to throw him the dress I'd been wearing, as he intended incorporating some of the features into his new models. That was the reason he was holding it when – when you passed. He was examining it, you see.'

'I could have strangled you! – and when, later, you said you were borrowing a thousand pounds—! I don't know how I kept my hands off you!'

'Don't heed it now,' she quivered. 'It's all explained.' The fearful little note in her voice registered and he instantly softened, embracing her tenderly.

'You mustn't tremble, my darling,' he whispered, his lips caressing her cheek. 'Don't ever be afraid, sweetheart, for I'll never hurt you again.'

'Nor I you,' she fervently responded. 'I don't deserve happiness such as this, Lean, for I was so very wicked.'

'Not wicked, just foolish – my mother tried to impress that upon me, because she liked you, Melanie.'

'She did – until she lost her money. Lean ... it was awful when she and Eleni stopped speaking to me.' In spite of herself tears fell on to her cheeks. Lean gently wiped them away with his handkerchief.

'They know the truth now.'

'Now? Already?'

'I telephoned them both – which reminds me, I'll have to phone them again first thing in the morning, or they won't be here for the wedding.'

The wedding. ... Melanie yawned and pressed

closer to him.

'I must go,' she said reluctantly at last. 'It's past one o'clock.'

'You mustn't go to that room,' he said remorsefully. 'I'll find you one of the best guest rooms.'

But she would not have it.

'It'll seem like a palace tonight,' she declared with a tender laugh, 'because I feel like a princess!' She turned at the door and his eyes swept adoringly over her.

'You look like one,' he responded huskily. 'My princess . . . I think that is what I shall call you. My English princess. . . .'

**Three of the world's greatest romance authors.
Don't miss any of this new series!**

ANNE HAMPSON

- ☐ #1 GATES OF STEEL
- ☐ #2 MASTER OF MOONROCK
- ☐ #7 DEAR STRANGER
- ☐ #10 WAVES OF FIRE
- ☐ #13 A KISS FROM SATAN
- ☐ #16 WINGS OF NIGHT

ANNE MATHER

- ☐ #3 SWEET REVENGE
- ☐ #4 THE PLEASURE & THE PAIN
- ☐ #8 THE SANCHEZ TRADITION
- ☐ #11 WHO RIDES THE TIGER
- ☐ #14 STORM IN A RAIN BARREL
- ☐ #17 LIVING WITH ADAM

VIOLET WINSPEAR

- ☐ #5 DEVIL IN A SILVER ROOM
- ☐ #6 THE HONEY IS BITTER
- ☐ #9 WIFE WITHOUT KISSES
- ☐ #12 DRAGON BAY
- ☐ #15 THE LITTLE NOBODY
- ☐ #18 THE KISSES AND THE WINE

To: HARLEQUIN READER SERVICE, Dept. N 308

M.P.O. Box 707, Niagara Falls, N.Y. 14302

Canadian address: Stratford, Ont., Canada

☐ Please send me the free Harlequin Romance Presents Catalogue.

☐ Please send me the titles checked.

I enclose $_____ (No C.O.D.'s). All books are 75c each. To help defray postage and handling cost, please add 25c.

Name _____

Address _____

City/Town _____

State/Prov. _____ Zip _____

N 308 P